A Journey of the Heart from

Broken to Beautiful

"An Imbalanced Life Is Just the Beginning of a Balanced One."

When she rose in her strength, Everything she once lost returned—quietly and

By: Dr. Gyaneshwari Dev Rakesh Kumar Sharma

Story Timeline: A highlight for readers

Introduction to main characters: "Meet Them Before Their Story Begins…"

□□ **Anjali Sharma**

The eldest daughter of the house.
An IAS officer with iron will and soft eyes.
She has walked through fire — not once, but many times —
and still managed to smile without asking for applause.
They call her Madam, but in silence,
She still craves the peace of being held without questions.
She is not the heroine.
She is the reason stories are born.

👶□ **Yatharva**

The child of hope.
Adopted by Anjali with the love of a thousand mothers.
Born of someone else's blood,
but raised through a bond stronger than biology.
He doesn't speak much, but he says everything.
His giggles healed the house.
His first steps were a revolution.

□□ **Vihan Pandit**

Once lost in ego,
now learning the art of repair.
He broke her once — perhaps twice —
but stayed long enough to pick up every piece.
He is not here to be forgiven easily,
but to prove that some men change…
and stay changed.
Quiet. Present. Willing.

👨‍👩‍👧‍👦 **Anjali's Family**

A blend of tradition and fierce love.
Her father: silent strength.
Her mother: the tear that never falls.

Her Tau ji: the calm in every storm.

And her sisters —
sharp-tongued, warm-hearted,
forever ready to protect their Didi,
but also the loudest laughers in the room.

🧳 The People Who Judged Her

They live on the margins of this story —
relatives, neighbors, so-called well-wishers.
They once broke her spirit.
Now, they will witness her rise.
Not as revenge.
But as redemption.

🏚 The Mansion

Not just a house — a witness.
It has seen tears under pillows,
and silent prayers in the pooja corner.
Walls that once echoed with doubt,
now hum with music, healing, and hope.
This home has character —
because it was broken too…
and rebuilt with love.

Chapter 1: The Dawn of Realization

In the quiet serenity of Vishranta , where the gentle river Sarasvati meandered through lush fields and ancient trees whispered stories of time, stood a young woman named Anjali . Her silhouette was framed against the dawn's soft golden hue, her eyes lost in the vast expanse of water and sky. She was dressed in a simple cotton saree, the fabric modest yet elegant, reflecting her humble beginnings and unwavering spirit.

Anjali had always been someone who believed in love's purity—yet her heart carried scars of unspoken pain. She had loved once, deeply and sincerely, with a devotion that knew no bounds. Her beloved, Vihaan, was a charming soul who once looked at her with tenderness, promising a future built on trust and mutual respect. But over time, Vihaan changed. His words grew colder, his actions more distant. He began to treat her with indifference, demanding compromises that chipped away at her dignity.

She remembered those days vividly—how she had given her heart entirely, refusing to betray her love even when others came with proposals, urging her to move on. She had received many offers, from well-meaning families and ambitious suitors, but her love for Vihaan had kept her faithful. The pain of separation had been inevitable—they had parted ways, not out of choice but because of circumstances beyond their control. Still, she had remained loyal, holding onto her self-respect and the hope that someday, he would see her worth again.

Now, years had passed since that painful goodbye. Anjali had grown into a woman of strength and purpose. She had studied diligently, her efforts earning her recognition and respect. She was on the cusp of achieving her dreams—she aimed to serve her country, to bring positive change as a future officer. Her journey was marked by perseverance, resilience, and an unbreakable belief in herself.

But sitting alone by the riverbank, Anjali couldn't help but revisit her past. Her mind drifted back to the days of innocence and love, the promises made beneath the same sky. She closed her eyes for a moment, feeling the cool breeze on her skin, recalling the warmth of Vihaan 's smile, and the ache of betrayal when he had turned away.

A tear escaped, tracing a path down her cheek, but her gaze was steady—her soul had learned to forgive, to heal, to move forward. She knew that her worth was not defined by her past heartbreak but by her strength to rise above it.

Suddenly, the peaceful silence was broken by a voice calling from behind. "Didi," called a soft, familiar voice— her younger sister .

"There's a call from Patna for you," she added anxiously.

"I asked him not to call on this number multiple times, but he is not ready to stop reaching out," she said, concern evident in her voice.

Anjali sighed softly, glancing at the river once more. Her heart was heavy with memories, yet her mind was clear. She stood up slowly, brushing the dust from her simple cotton saree, and turned to face her sister.

"Let it be," she replied quietly, a newfound resolve in her voice. "Some calls are meant to be ignored. I have my own path now."

As she walked away from the riverbank, the rising sun cast long shadows behind her, symbolizing the dawn of a new chapter in her life—

one where she would forge her destiny, guided by resilience, dignity, and hope.

Chapter 2: The Dawn of New Responsibilities

After leaving the riverbank, **Anjali** took a deep breath, feeling the cool morning air fill her lungs. The sun had already begun its ascent, casting a warm glow over the village. Today marked a new beginning—she was posted as an IAS officer just last week in the very district where she had grown up. The weight of her responsibilities had not yet fully settled, but her resolve was firm.

She moved swiftly, preparing herself for the day ahead. She tied her long hair neatly and placed a simple black bindi on her forehead—a symbol of her cultural roots and her strength. Her saree was a bright yellow, a color that reflected hope, energy, and renewal. She dressed with care, knowing that every detail mattered when stepping into a role that would shape her future and serve her community.

She sat at the breakfast table, the aroma of freshly cooked food filling the modest home. The maid, a kind woman who had known Anjali since childhood, was serving her a plate of parathas and fresh fruit. Just as Anjali was about to take her first bite, the phone on the table rang sharply, slicing through the quiet morning.

The maid glanced at the caller ID and her eyes widened slightly. **"Didi,"** she said softly, **"this is the same number. I have told you about it before."**

Anjali paused, her hand hovering over her plate. She looked at the screen, her mind racing—whose name or number could it be? She reached out and picked up the phone with a calm but cautious demeanor.

"Hello," she said, her voice steady, yet expectant.

For a moment, there was silence on the other end. Then, a voice—faint, familiar, and unmistakably his—caused her to freeze. The world seemed to stand still as her eyes widened in disbelief. She stood abruptly, her hand gripping the phone tightly, her heart pounding.

It was him.

Vihaan.

Anjali's breath caught in her throat. The voice on the other end was familiar—soft yet laden with emotion, carrying memories she had tried to bury deep within her heart. Her fingers trembled slightly as she held the phone tightly, her mind racing with a thousand thoughts.

For a moment, she simply stood there, rooted to the spot, eyes fixed on the horizon outside the window but her mind elsewhere. Her heart pounded loudly in her chest, each beat echoing the tumult of emotions—shock, anger, longing, and a strange flicker of hope.

Vihaan's voice broke the silence, tentative but pleading.
"Anjali... I know it's been long. I... I just wanted to hear your voice."

The words hung in the air, heavy with unspoken memories. Anjali's breath hitched, and she felt a surge of conflicting feelings. Her mind flashed back to the pain, the disrespect, the love she had once given without hesitation—now turned into a distant echo.

She closed her eyes briefly, trying to steady herself. Her voice, when she finally spoke, was calm but firm.
"Vihaan," she said softly, **"why are you calling? After all this time?"**

There was a pause on the other end, then his voice, a little more hesitant.
"I... I just wanted to check on you. I've been trying to reach you for days."

Anjali took a deep breath. The gentle morning breeze seemed to carry her words now, cutting through the lingering past.
"I have moved on, Vihaan. I have responsibilities now. My life has changed."

A silence stretched between them. She could hear him shifting nervously, perhaps realizing the weight of his own actions, or the consequences of his silence all these years.

Her eyes clouded with emotion, but she kept her voice steady.
"It's better we don't speak anymore. I am where I am because I chose

to be true to myself. I wish you well, but I need to focus on my work now."

With that, she gently placed the phone down on the table, her hand trembling slightly. Her heart was pounding fiercely—yet, somewhere inside, a newfound strength blossomed. She had faced heartbreak, betrayal, and disappointment, but she was still standing tall.

As she looked out the window, the rising sun bathed her in a golden glow—a symbol of her awakening, her new beginning.

Chapter 3: The Rise of a New Dawn

As the first light of dawn faded into the bright morning, **Anjali** stepped out of her modest home, now transformed into a symbol of her new journey. Several sleek, black cars with sirens and flags followed her, a sign of her new stature as the district's **IAS officer**. Her every move radiated dignity and confidence, a reflection of her unwavering resolve and the respect she had earned through her perseverance.

She approached the grand office complex, a sprawling building that housed the district collectorate. With calm authority, she entered, her saree perfectly draped, her demeanor composed. Her eyes held the calm of someone who had faced storms and emerged stronger.

In her office, she took a moment to inform her mother over the phone. **"Ma, I've reached the office now. Everything is in order. I will keep you updated,"** she said softly, her voice echoing with pride and responsibility.

Her secretary, a young woman with a bright smile, approached her with a note.
"Madam, you're invited to a university for a lecture. They want your insights on development and gender equality."

Anjali nodded thoughtfully.
"Arrange for me to go. I will leave soon."

Later that day, dressed in a crisp suit that complemented her vibrant saree, **Anjali** arrived at the university—one of the most prestigious institutions in the country. The auditorium was packed with students, scholars, and dignitaries from around the world. The atmosphere buzzed with anticipation.

She was introduced as a distinguished scholar, a woman who had excelled in history before dedicating herself to public service. Her reputation preceded her, and the audience listened intently as she stepped onto the podium.

With clarity, passion, and authority, she addressed the gathering. **"Today, we stand at a crossroads. Our rivers—lifelines of our land—are suffering. The revival of river canals is vital—not just for irrigation but for sustainable development, for our environment, and for future generations. Equally important is gender equality—empowering women is not just a moral duty but a necessity for a resilient society."**

Her words resonated deeply with everyone present. She spoke of the importance of restoring natural resources, fostering equality, and harnessing the collective strength of her nation.

When she finished, the applause was thunderous. Her speech was shared widely on social media, newspapers, and within academic circles. She was praised as an inspiring leader who combined her scholarly background with her commitment to public welfare.

From that day on, **Anjali's** reputation soared beyond her district. She became a symbol of hope and change—a woman who was not afraid to speak truth to power, who believed in progress for all.

Her journey from a humble village girl to a respected officer, scholar, and advocate for change had only just begun.

As **Anjali** concluded her speech and stepped down from the podium, a young man in the crowd pushed forward slightly, eager to speak. He had been following her work since his graduation—an admirer of her articles, her insights, and her unwavering dedication. Today, he finally had the chance to meet her in person.

"Ma'am," he began hesitantly, clutching a notebook filled with notes and references. **"I've read many of your articles—especially those about education and social reform. They truly inspired me."**

Anjali smiled kindly, encouraging him to speak.

"It's all about education, ma'am," he continued passionately. **"But if you don't mind, I have a personal question. Why are you not married yet? Have you ever been in love?"**

The question was unexpected, but the atmosphere was live, streamed on the university's official page, with viewers worldwide. The room grew silent, awaiting her response. Even **Vihaan**, watching from afar, paused to listen.

Anjali's eyes flickered with a mixture of amusement and calm composure. She looked at the young man and then to the camera, her voice steady and measured.
"Sabke apne gam hain, hamare kuch kam hain," she said softly, a gentle smile touching her lips. (Translation: "Everyone has their own sorrows, and I have my own burdens.")
"Let's not talk about this page of my life," she added, her tone light yet firm.

A moment of silence followed as she gracefully excused herself, leaving the young scholar and the audience pondering her words. She walked away, her steps confident and poised, leaving behind an impression of strength and dignity.

The livestream continued, viewers captivated by her graceful handling of personal questions, and her message of resilience spread even further. **Anjali**, in that simple yet profound response, conveyed a truth: her life was her own story—one written with perseverance, dignity, and purpose.

As she disappeared into the corridors of her office complex, the world saw her not just as a government officer, but as a beacon of inspiration—someone who carried her past with grace and faced her future with unwavering resolve.

Chapter 4: Shadows of the Past

As the sun dipped below the horizon, casting a golden hue over **Vishranta**, **Anjali** wrapped up her day's work. Her mind was still preoccupied, her thoughts drifting back to the conversation during the live conference—the personal question that had made her pause. The question about her marriage and love had lingered in her mind, stirring a mix of emotions she had long tried to suppress.

She looked at her phone once more, its screen glowing softly in the dim light of her office. Her fingers hovered over it, her heart fluttering with memories and unresolved feelings. The day's work had been fulfilling, yet her mind kept returning to her past with **Vihaan**.

Later that evening, seeking solace, she left her office and headed home. The sky had opened up, and rain began to fall gently, its rhythmic patter creating a soothing sound. She found refuge in her small cottage within the residency garden, sitting on a wooden bench with a cup of tea in her hand. The rain washed over her like a cleansing wave, yet her mind was far from peaceful.

She stared into the swirling drops, her thoughts drifting to her past with **Vihaan**—the man she had loved with all her heart, and the pain she had endured because of him. She remembered how much she had given him, how she had sacrificed her dignity to keep the love alive. She had ignored her self-respect, endured insults from his family, and faced his anger and shouting—all in the hope that he would see her worth.

"I destroyed my own dignity for him," she whispered softly to herself, her voice trembling slightly.
"I begged him to stay, to love me, even when he disrespected me again and again."

Her mind replayed the moments when she tried to talk sense, when she pleaded with him to understand her feelings. How she had stood by him, hoping that someday he would value her true worth. But all her efforts seemed to fall on deaf ears. His indifference, his dismissiveness, and the hurtful words from his family had left scars that she thought would never heal.

"It's been five years," she murmured, her eyes moist, **"no contact, no regrets, no tears. I've been busy, I've moved on."** Yet, deep inside, a part of her still yearned for closure, for peace.

Just then, her phone buzzed again—an incoming call. Her heart skipped a beat. It was him.

"Vihaan," she thought, her fingers trembling as she looked at the screen.

She hesitated, then answered.

"Please," his voice pleaded on the other end, trembling with desperation. **"Don't hang up. Please, don't cut the call. I… I am sorry for everything. I was wrong. I didn't value you, I didn't understand what I had. Please forgive me."**

Her heart clenched. The flood of old emotions threatened to overwhelm her. She felt herself wavering, the weak girl she once was trying to reemerge. But she took a deep breath, steadying herself.

"Vihaan," she said softly but firmly, **"I have moved on. I have rebuilt my life, my dignity. I cannot go back to what was. Please understand—I deserve respect. Please don't call again."**

There was a long pause. Then, unexpectedly, he started to cry—begging, pleading, apologizing profusely.
"I was a fool. I was blind. I promise, I will change. Just… don't end everything like this."

Anjali closed her eyes, feeling the weight of her past and present collide. She knew that her strength had been tested many times, and each time she had risen, stronger than before. This moment was no different.

"Goodbye, Vihaan," she whispered into the phone, her voice calm but resolute. **"Some wounds take time to heal, and some hearts need to heal alone. I wish you well. Please respect my decision."**

With a final click, she ended the call, letting the rain wash away the lingering tears. She sat silently for a moment, gazing at the falling droplets, her mind poised on the edge of the future—determined not to let her past define her anymore.

"No more weakness," she whispered to herself. **"I am enough."**

Just as **Anjali** was trying to regain her composure, her phone vibrated again. Her heart sank as she saw the caller ID—**Vihaan**. A wave of anger and pain surged through her as she snatched the phone, her hands trembling.

"Why are you calling again?" she shouted into the phone, voice rising with frustration and helplessness. **"What's your problem? Why don't you leave me alone—just like you did all those years ago?"**

There was a brief silence on the other end, then his trembling voice. **"Sorry, Anjali. I am sorry. I didn't mean to hurt you."**

But she cut him off sharply, voice trembling with a mixture of rage and heartbreak.
"No! Ooooooo, no! Sorry doesn't work anymore, Vihaan. This is not how things work. Do you think it's fun—leaving your love, feeling your love slipping away, blaming me for things I never even did?"

Her voice cracked, but her words poured out with the raw emotion that had been bottled up for years.
"I know now—you're coming back because everyone around you has betrayed you. All those loved ones—your friends, your family—they must have cheated on you. Now you feel that everyone is selfish. I was right all along when I said you need to understand who is truly yours and who is not."

The tears she had fought so hard to hold back threatened to spill over, but she pressed on, voice fierce and unwavering.
"Let me tell you, that wasn't just a mistake. That was a blunder—a huge mistake that shattered everything we had. Please, don't disturb me anymore."

He begged on the other end, voice breaking into sobs.
"Sorry, Anjali. I promise, I'll never call again."

But her heart, hardened by years of pain, refused to soften this time. Instead of pleading like she did five years ago, she shouted with all her strength.
"No! No more goodbyes, no more apologies. It's been so long, and I was finally feeling better—until you showed up and shattered me again." Her voice trembled, but she refused to let her tears fall.
"Congratulations, Vihaan. You've won again."

His voice grew more desperate, crying louder.
"Sorry! Sorry! Please forgive me, I didn't mean to hurt you—"

But she cut him off, her voice rising even louder.
"Enough! Just go. Leave me alone."

She ended the call with a heavy sigh, feeling the familiar old ache surge through her. Her knees felt weak, and she sank back on the bench, her hands trembling. Her mind was flooded with memories of the final breakup, the heartbreak, and the tears she had shed then.

Slowly, she took a deep breath, drank some water, and tried to steady herself. When she looked up again, her voice was calmer but tinged with a new resolve.

"Leave it. Tell me—are you okay now? Are you doing fine?" she asked softly, her eyes searching.

There was a long pause. Then, her voice softened as she heard his reply.
"Everything's falling apart. I'm all alone. No one is by my side anymore."

She listened quietly, recognizing the loneliness behind his words. For a moment, she felt a pang of pity, but her inner strength quickly overshadowed it.

"It's your own doing," she said gently. **"You can't keep running from your mistakes. But I hope you find what you're looking for—somewhere out there."**

She ended the call, her mind exhausted but her spirit unbroken. The rain continued to fall softly, washing away the remnants of her pain as she sat in silence, contemplating her journey—her strength, her resilience, and her unwavering resolve to move forward.

Chapter 5: A Day of Reflection

It was a peaceful Sunday morning. The soft rays of the sun filtered through the curtains, casting a gentle glow across her room. **Anjali** woke up naturally, feeling the calmness that Sundays brought—a break from her hectic routine, a moment to reflect and recharge.

She began her day with her usual exercise—stretching, yoga, and breathing exercises that helped clear her mind. The quiet discipline of her morning routine gave her a sense of grounding, a reminder of her strength and resilience. After her physical practice, she performed her daily **puja** and **paath**—a ritual that connected her to her roots, her faith, and the inner peace she sought.

Once her prayers were complete, she sat down for a simple breakfast—fresh fruits, warm parathas, and a cup of steaming tea. Her mind wandered to her mother, whom she called regularly to share her thoughts and seek comfort. She picked up her phone and dialed her mother's number, hearing her warm voice on the other end.

"Ma," she said softly, **"I'm doing well. Just the usual work. How are you?"**

Her mother's voice was filled with concern and love.
"Beta, you've become so strong. I am proud of you. Remember, no matter how tough things get, always stay true to yourself."

They exchanged a few more words, sharing small updates and blessings. After hanging up, Anjali looked at her phone again. Her fingers hesitated over the screen. Thoughts flooded her mind—memories of his last call, the pain, the longing, and her own internal debate.

"Should I call him back?" she thought, her heart heavy. **"Maybe he is really in need. Maybe he's truly sorry this time."**

Her mind was a battlefield—her instincts told her to stay away, to protect herself from further hurt. But her compassion, her empathy, whispered that perhaps, just perhaps, she should hear him out, understand his pain, and see if there was any hope left.

She stared at the phone, her finger hovering over the call button. Her heart pounded louder with each passing second—thoughts swirling in her mind:
What if he's genuinely sorry?
What if he's changed?
Can I just listen, even if I don't want to forgive?

Finally, after a long moment of silence, she pressed the call button.

On the banks of the serene Ganges in **Rishikesh**, **Vihaan** was sitting quietly, lost in the tranquil beauty of the place. The sound of flowing water and distant chants created a peaceful atmosphere, but nothing compared to the storm of emotions raging inside him. His phone suddenly vibrated, and when he saw her name flashing on the screen, his heart leapt with joy.

"Anjali," he whispered softly, a broad smile spreading across his face. It had been over five years since they last spoke, and in that moment, he felt the happiest he had in a very long time—probably the happiest since he had lost her.

Without hesitation, he answered eagerly, almost trembling with excitement.
"Hello?"

Her voice came through, calm yet with a hint of resolve.

But instead of continuing with her usual cautious tone, he launched into a flood of words—his voice filled with gratitude and longing.
"Anjali, I am so happy you called. Honestly, I've been waiting for this moment for a long time. I don't even know how to thank you for picking up the call today. It means everything to me."

He paused, trying to gather himself, then continued with a tone of heartfelt regret.
"I've realized so much over these years—how much I took you for granted, how much I hurt you, and how blind I was to your worth. I am truly sorry for all the pain I caused you, for every insult, every anger, every selfish act. I was wrong—completely wrong."

His voice cracked with emotion.
"Please forgive me, Anjali. I've been lost without you, and I regret every moment I let you go. I know I don't deserve your forgiveness easily, but I want you to know that I am genuinely sorry. I wish I could turn back time and undo everything."

On the other end, **Anjali** listened quietly. Her heart was pounding—her mind a whirl of conflicting feelings. She could hear the sincerity in his voice, but her own pain and scars made her cautious. Still, she remained silent for a moment, allowing herself to process his words.

"Vihaan," she finally said softly, **"I've heard your words. And maybe, just maybe, I needed to hear this today."** Her voice was steady but lacked the warmth it once held. **"But you must understand—words are easy. Actions speak louder. I've moved on, and I cannot forget everything so easily. What matters now is what you do moving forward."**

There was a long pause. He was still on the line, silent, remorseful.

"Thank you for calling," she said softly, her voice gentle but firm. **"Please take care of yourself. That's all I want."**

He replied with a faint voice, **"Thanks."**

She hesitated for a moment, then asked softly, **"Ok now, tell me—what happened? Are you okay?"**

There was a long pause, then his voice broke as he started to speak, overwhelmed with emotion.
"Anjali, I was fighting with my relatives. They kept blaming me for all their losses, for everything that went wrong. Later, I found out they defamed me in society—said I was characterless, that I had no morals. I used to think they were my family, that they could never be wrong. But you were right all along."

His voice quivered with pain.
"They secretly transferred all my parents' property into their names—got my signatures on papers I never read properly. I was

blind, I was wrong about their feelings. I never knew they could be so selfish."

He paused, voice choking with emotion.
"The lady who insulted you—she slapped my mother and father too. She was so mannerless, she abused my brother and his wife. She insulted me so badly. I never imagined she'd do all this."

His voice cracked as tears came through.
"It was my birthday, and she asked me to leave. If she had asked me gently, I wouldn't have said a word. But she insulted me, just like she did with you—publicly, humiliating us all."

Anjali's eyes welled with tears as she listened. Her heart ached for him, for all the pain he had endured. But she quickly steadied herself, gathering courage.
"No worries, Vihaan," she said softly, trying to console him. **"Finally, you've come to know the truth. That's good. Now tell me—how are uncle and aunty? And the other members?"**

He sighed deeply, voice heavy with regret.
"They all blame me now. They think I am responsible for everything. Maybe they're right. Like you warned me before, I never paid attention. I never thought they could do this to me."

He started crying again, voice trembling.
"Anjali, I am totally exhausted. I don't know what to do anymore."

She closed her eyes for a moment, then spoke calmingly.
"Relax, Vihaan. Where are you now?"

"In Rishikesh, at the bank of the Ganga—just arrived this morning," he replied softly.

"Good," she said gently. **"Drink some water. Take a deep breath. Just breathe. Things will get better. You need to stay strong."**

He sniffled, then replied **"I have no Idea, What should I do? How do I get it back? Currently,My brother is dealing with them "**

She listened carefully, and replied, OK let him handle this else you can give him my number, will get this done .

He took a deep breath, trying to regain his composure. **"Thanks, Anjali. Honestly, I don't know what I'd do without you. You're the only one who's been there for me."**

She responded softly, **"You're not alone anymore. Just remember, it's important to stay calm and focused. Everything will fall into place."**

She asked, By the Way, what about your career? What are you doing these days?

He Replied calmly, For now I am **good in job, In previous days, that's the only thing I have been good at—still in the same field as before, and promoted to Sr. Manager.**

"Just keep your focus. Things will work out. You need patience and clarity. Don't let this chaos pull you down," Anjali said softly, her voice soothing yet firm. She added with warmth, **"You can always count on me. Just relax and go home safely."**

Vihaan's voice trembled with gratitude, thick with tears. **"Thank you, Anjali. Really. You're the only one who's been there for me. I… I don't know what I'd do without you."** His heavy voice conveyed the weight of regret and hope, however fragile it was.

She listened patiently, then gently replied, **"Take care of yourself. Remember, you're not alone anymore. Keep faith. Everything will fall into place."**

As she ended the call, her mind was already drifting back to her routine, but she felt a strange warmth—hope flickering faintly in her heart despite all the pain.

Just then, her maid's voice interrupted her thoughts. **"Didi, the lawyer is calling you. We can go to get our baby this Monday,"** she announced happily.

Anjali's face lit up instantly. A rush of excitement flooded her. **"Oh! That's wonderful,"** she exclaimed, a bright smile spreading across her face. **"I'll talk to the lawyer now."** Without hesitation, she quickly dropped the phone, eager to make arrangements for the upcoming visit.

Her heart fluttered with anticipation, the thought of holding her child again filling her with renewed hope. She knew this was a step toward healing, toward moving forward in her life.

Vihaan, meanwhile, listened to her words and felt a ripple of curiosity and anxiety. **"Who is this baby?"** he wondered silently, a twinge of suspicion stirring within him. **"Does she have someone else now? Or… is this another part of her life I don't know about?"**

The last lines of her conversation echoed in his mind—her reassurance to him, her kindness, and her strength. Despite everything, he realized that the bond they once shared was not entirely broken. It was fragile, yes, but still present. Anjali's resilience and the new hope she carried within her left a faint but unmistakable mark on his heart.

As the day moved forward, both of them carried the weight of their past and the uncertain promise of their future—one filled with hope, regret, and the possibility of new beginnings.

Chapter 6: A Step Forward and a Rainy Reflection

Anjali arrived at the lawyer's office with a mixture of impatience and hope. As she sat across the table, the lawyer looked at her with a gentle, reassuring smile.

"There's a delay in the process of getting the baby," he said softly. **"The application has been pending, and the court is taking time. It's been over a year now."**

She took a deep breath, feeling the familiar frustration rise within her. **"I've been waiting so long,"** she said quietly, her voice steady but edged with longing. **"It's been a year, and still no sign of progress."**

The lawyer nodded understandingly.
"Relax, Anjali. You know how patient you've been throughout this journey. We will make this happen. It's just about a week more. Trust me."

Her shoulders eased slightly, and she nodded in agreement. **"Okay, I trust you."**

She left the office with a renewed sense of hope, her mind already shifting to her next plan—spending quality time with her family.

Later that day, she visited her parents and sisters. The house was filled with warmth and the familiar aroma of home-cooked food. She sat with her father, uncles, and mother, sharing stories from her childhood, reminiscing about simpler days and the innocence of her early years.

Her father and uncle, always eager to see her settled and happy, again broached the subject she had long avoided.
"Anjali, isn't it possible that you could get married now? You've worked so hard, and maybe it's time to think about your own happiness."

She smiled politely, choosing to skip that topic for the moment. Instead, she talked about her responsibilities at work, her plans to strengthen her district, and her desire to spend more time with her family.

Inspired by her newfound hope, she proposed a family trip—**a pilgrimage to the 12 Jyotirlingas**—a spiritual journey she had longed for. Her family enthusiastically agreed, and they set the date. They traveled together, visiting the sacred sites peacefully and safely, cherishing every moment of togetherness after so long apart.

When the trip concluded, she returned to her district, returning to her office work with renewed energy. The responsibilities of her role weighed on her, but her spirit was lighter.

It was a bright morning, and she was leaving from a Tehsil Diwas event, riding in her car, when suddenly, the sky darkened. Thick clouds gathered, and soon, rain began pouring down in heavy droplets.

She looked out of the window, watching the rain cascade over the fields and trees. Without hesitation, she asked the driver, **"Stop the car."**

The driver slowed down and pulled over to the side of the road. She stepped out into the rain, feeling the cool drops wash over her face and hair. She stood there silently for a moment, taking in the refreshing scent of wet earth and the rhythmic sound of rain falling all around.

Her car was parked nearby, and the other officials had already left for their offices. She stayed alone with her driver and the car, feeling the rain seep into her soul.

She closed her eyes and took a deep breath, then walked a few steps to the roadside stall where an old man was preparing tea with ginger and elaichi—cardamom.

"Bhaiya, do cup chai,"(Two cups of tea) she said softly, smiling as she watched him prepare the steaming drink. When the tea was ready, she took a sip, savoring the warmth and aroma.

As she sipped her tea, her mind drifted to memories of simpler times—those mornings when she and Vihaan used to go out for "nukkad wali chai," sharing quiet conversations and enjoying the rain. A gentle smile formed on her lips as she remembered those moments.

While lost in her thoughts, her phone buzzed. She looked at the screen—it was a message from him.

"Sorry for the disturbance, but can we meet, please? Just once. I know it's been tough for you, and my sudden appearance might hurt, but you are always strong. I miss you every day. I just want to see you."

Her hand trembled slightly as she stared at the message. She hesitated, then slowly picked up the phone, took a deep breath, and decided to reply.

With a calm, steady tone, she typed: **"OK. Meet me the day after tomorrow. I will book your flight tickets. My driver will pick you up."**

After sending the message, she looked out again at the rain, feeling a strange mix of nostalgia and resolve. Her heart, despite everything, was quietly hopeful.

As she watched the rain cascade down, a quiet thought crept into her mind—one she had been avoiding for days. It was a gnawing feeling that refused to go away.

"It's been more than a month," she thought, her brow furrowing as she recalled the silence from the lawyer's office. Despite her repeated inquiries and hopes, there had been no update, no response.

Her heart sank with a mixture of frustration and disappointment. She had held onto this dream of finally holding her child, of completing her family, with unwavering faith. But now, doubts crept in—**was it time to accept that perhaps her hope was slipping away?**

She took a deep breath, feeling the cool air fill her lungs, and made a silent decision.

"I will have one final discussion with the lawyer," she thought firmly. **"Either I get clarity today, or I let go of this dream altogether."**

The rain continued to fall softly around her, as if echoing her resolve. She pulled out her phone and dialed the lawyer's number.

After a few rings, he answered, his voice still gentle but with a hint of regret.
"Hello, Anjali."

She cut straight to the point.
"It's been over a month. I need to know—what's the status of the court case? Are we making any progress?"

There was a pause on the other end. The lawyer hesitated, then spoke slowly.
"I'm sorry, ma'am. The process is still pending. There are some legal hurdles, and the court's backlog is quite long."

She listened quietly, feeling the weight of those words. Her heart sank a little, but she kept her tone steady.
"I see. I've waited patiently, but I cannot keep waiting forever. I need a clear answer. Do I keep believing, or should I accept that my dream might not come true?"

The lawyer sighed softly.
"I understand, ma'am. I will try to expedite the process. But I can't promise an immediate result."

She took a deep breath, the sound of rain soothing yet grounding her.
"Thank you," she said softly. **"This will be my last attempt. If I don't hear anything soon, I will have to accept that it's time to move on."**

She ended the call, feeling a strange mix of relief and sadness. She looked once more at the pouring rain, a symbol of cleansing and new beginnings, but also of the acceptance she needed to make.

"Maybe," she whispered to herself, **"it's time to let go of the dream that has kept me going. I must focus on the life I am building—on the love I have in my family, and the hope I nurture every day."**

With that resolve, she turned away from the roadside stall, her heart a little lighter, yet stronger. The rain had washed away her doubts, and now she was ready to face whatever lay ahead—alone but not defeated.

Chapter 7: Embracing the Present, Letting Go of the Past

The day was bright, but her heart was steady and composed as she prepared to meet **Vihaan**. She knew this encounter would bring back memories, but she was determined to face it with dignity and focus on her future.

When she arrived at the designated place, Vihaan was already waiting. His face showed signs of exhaustion, regret, and hope, but her expression remained calm and unwavering.

"Vihaan," she greeted softly but firmly, her tone unwavering.

He looked up, eyes filled with remorse and longing.
"Anjali, I'm sorry… for everything. For the pain, for the hurt. I was wrong—so wrong."

She listened quietly, then responded with quiet strength.
"Your apologies are accepted. But I want you to understand—there's no hope to restart what we had. I am focused on the present now. I have moved on, and I am building my life."

Her words were clear, her voice steady.
"You need to continue and move on too. Life is too precious to hold onto the past."

He looked down, remorse washing over him, then asked hesitantly,
"And… the baby? I heard you mention it during the call. Who is he? Is he…?"

She nodded gently, her eyes softening.
"That is the baby I am trying to adopt. It's been a long journey, but I am hopeful. I want to give him a good life, a life full of love and stability."

Vihaan's eyes widened as he absorbed her words. A strange sense of relief washed over him—realizing she was not in a relationship, not involved with anyone else. It was a small but significant sign that she was truly focused on her new chapter.

"That's good," he whispered softly, a faint smile forming. **"I'm glad to hear that. I'm happy for you, Anjali."**

Suddenly, her phone buzzed loudly, breaking the moment. She looked at the screen—it was the lawyer. Her face lit up instantly.

"We need to leave—right now," she exclaimed, excitement bubbling in her voice. **"The lawyer says everything is finalized. We have to go and get the baby."**

Without wasting a second, she called her parents, her voice filled with joy.
"Mom, Dad, it's happening! The court has approved the adoption. We're going to bring him home today."

Her parents cheered, their happiness evident even over the phone. Her sisters shared their excitement, and the entire family was filled with joy and anticipation.

Vihaan looked on, a mixture of happiness for her and a quiet hope that she would find the happiness she deserved.

They all hurried to the place where the baby boy was waiting. When they finally saw him—small, innocent, with bright eyes—they knew he was the missing piece of her life.

She gently picked him up, holding him close, her heart swelling with love. She looked into his tiny face and made a decision.
"Yatharva," she whispered softly, **"because you are the only one who can complete me. You are the gift I've waited for all my life."**

In that moment, surrounded by her family and her new son, she felt a sense of peace. Her past was behind her, her focus was on the present, and her future was bright with hope and love.

Because sometimes, the right person—no matter how small—was enough to make everything complete.

And **Yatharva** was that hope for her, her reason to smile each day, her reason to believe in a better tomorrow.

Days turned into weeks. Anjali's life slowly settled into a new rhythm—one filled with lullabies, midnight feedings, and baby giggles that echoed through her home like blessings. The house that once felt too quiet now breathed with the gentle sounds of new life.

Yatharva had blended into the family like he had always belonged. Her parents couldn't stop spoiling him. Her sisters were obsessed with his every little sneeze, blink, and burp. And somewhere amidst all this joy, there was someone unexpected who kept showing up—Vihaan.

He started by offering small help—bringing diapers, asking if she needed anything, texting to check on the baby's health. At first, Anjali hesitated. She had drawn a line, and she intended to keep it. But something about the way Vihaan looked at Yatharva—softly, curiously, like a man discovering something sacred—made her pause.

One afternoon, she caught him sitting on the floor, cradling Yatharva in his arms. He was humming a lullaby—completely unaware she was watching from the doorway. The way he gently ran his finger across the baby's cheek, the way his smile widened when Yatharva cooed back—it wasn't forced. It wasn't about proving anything.

He wasn't pretending.

In the weeks that followed, Vihaan became a frequent presence—not as a lover trying to return, but as a friend. As someone who, perhaps for the first time, truly wanted to give rather than take. He began accompanying her to doctor visits, volunteering to watch the baby when she needed some rest, and sometimes just showing up with homemade food when she forgot to eat.

Anjali noticed. She saw the change. But she said nothing. She didn't encourage hope, but she didn't shut the door either. Because deep inside, she knew—people change, and not always for the worst.

A month passed since Yatharva entered her life. One quiet evening, as she sat on the balcony, Yatharva asleep on her chest, Vihaan sat beside her. The sky was painted with soft shades of pink and orange, like life itself was offering a new beginning.

“I never knew I could feel this kind of peace,” Vihaan said, his voice calm. “When I look at him, Anjali, I don’t see someone else’s child. I see… hope. A chance to do something right. Even if it’s from a distance.”

She looked at him—not with judgment, not with confusion, but with quiet understanding.

“I see it too,” she replied softly. “But this is his story now. Not ours. And if you want to be in it, it has to be with no expectations, no rewrites. Just honesty.”

He nodded, his gaze steady. “That’s all I want. To be a part of something good, even if it's just in the background.”

They sat in silence after that. Not awkward silence—just peaceful. Complete.

Because sometimes, healing doesn’t mean going back to what was. It means finding new roles in each other's lives, discovering new definitions of love, family, and redemption.

And as Anjali looked at her sleeping son, she smiled—not because everything was perfect, but because for the first time, it felt right.

Yatharva stirred a little in his sleep, and she whispered to him gently, “We’re okay, baby. We’re more than okay.”

Chapter 8: Confusion Under Moonlight

The nights had grown quieter, but Vihaan's heart had become louder than ever.

It had been over a month since Yatharva had entered their lives, and every day, Vihaan found himself slipping deeper into something he thought he had let go of—his feelings for Anjali. But this time, it wasn't the infatuation of youth. This wasn't about old memories or faded love. This was different—grounded, mature, and painfully honest.

He watched her from a distance, often during those moments when she wasn't aware—her hair tied messily while feeding the baby, her tired eyes still glowing with purpose after a full day at work, or how she'd sit late at night studying case files, balancing being a new mother and an IAS officer with effortless grace.

She had built a life. A strong, dignified, inspiring life.

And he… had only watched.

One night, he sat on the terrace alone. The stars were out, and the breeze was light, but his thoughts were anything but. He held his phone in his hand, staring at her contact name—*Anjali (Yatharva's Mumma)*. A smile tugged at his lips… and then vanished, replaced by a heavy sigh.

"How do you tell someone," he whispered to the wind, "that you love them, but you're not asking for a second chance? That you're proud of them, but ashamed of yourself?"

The truth gnawed at him.

He had hurt her in the past. Lied. Disrespected her trust. Back then, he didn't realize what he had, and by the time he did, it was too late. She had risen like a phoenix, and he had remained stuck in the smoke of his regrets.

But now, she was an IAS officer. A woman of strength, discipline, and kindness. And most importantly, a mother to a beautiful child. She didn't *need* him. That was the hardest part. She had moved on… and she had won.

And he? He was still carrying the guilt.

That's why he had made a decision.

He would speak to her. Not to win her back. But to free himself from the guilt that choked him every time she smiled politely, every time she thanked him for helping, and every time she looked at him with kindness, kindness he felt he didn't deserve.

He rehearsed his words in his head a dozen times.

"Anjali, I know we've become friends again… but there's something I need to tell you."

"I'm not here to confuse your life. I know where we stand. I just want you to know that I see who you are today—and I admire it."

"I also want to apologize… truly. Not to undo the past, but to stop it from haunting me. I was wrong, Anjali. I didn't just lose a girlfriend. I lost a woman who could've taught me how to be a better man."

And maybe… just maybe, he'd end with:

"You're getting marriage proposals now. You've become someone that people look up to. And if you ever find someone who deserves you, I'll be the first to smile—even if I'm hurting inside."

That was the truth. He wouldn't confess to get her back.

He'd confess… to set her free from his shadow. And maybe set himself free, too.

Because sometimes, the bravest kind of love is the one that asks for *nothing* in return.

Sleep didn't come to him that night. Vihaan lay awake, staring into the darkness, his mind spinning endlessly around one thought — *Anjali.* Her calm voice, her unshakable confidence, the way she handled everything around her. She had moved on. She had built a life that didn't need anyone, especially not someone who once broke her.

And yet, he couldn't stop himself.

"I'm going to propose to her," he whispered to himself in the silence. "She deserves to know how I feel… how much I've changed."

He thought about doing it on her birthday — maybe she'd smile, maybe it would be the perfect moment. No. That would look like he was using the day, trying to wrap his feelings in a celebration. It would feel like a trick.

"Maybe I should just call her… tell her everything."
But again, his heart said no. She would think it's casual. Like he wasn't serious — just like before.

"I'll take her out to dinner… talk to her face-to-face."
But there wasn't enough time. Everything she had helped him with was sorted now. There was no excuse to stay longer.

He was running out of time. And out of chances.

He went to the market the next morning, trying to clear his head. While scrolling through his phone, he got a call from their mutual friend, Ronie. Without thinking, he answered.

"What's going on, bro?" Ronie asked casually.

But Vihaan couldn't hide it anymore. He spilled everything — the thoughts, the guilt, the love that never really left.

"I want her back, Ronie. I want to propose to her. I want to be in her life. Forever."

There was silence. Then Ronie's voice changed. It wasn't casual anymore. It was real. Honest.

"Vihaan, you did wrong. You underestimated her… her love, her strength, her loyalty. You broke something deep inside her. If you truly want her back, you have to prove to her — not just that you love her, but that you've changed completely."

"I have changed," Vihaan replied quickly. "I'm a vegetarian now. No drinking, no bad language. I've taken trips just to learn how to control my anger. I'm not that guy anymore. I've become everything she ever asked me to be."

"But I'm scared, man. What if she doesn't see it? What if… she doesn't want me anymore? She's doing so well. She's complete, Ronie. Like a queen who never needed a king. But I still want her. I want her more now than ever. I want to rewrite our love story."

Ronie sighed.
"Listen, Vihaan. If you still want her, you have to be ready for pain. This won't be easy. First, you apologise — not just for the past, but for not standing by her when she needed it most. Tell her you were immature back then. That you didn't have the wisdom to see where she was right, and where the world was wrong."

"Tell her that now, after everything you've witnessed, you understand her pain. Tell her you'll never let her feel alone again. And most importantly, tell her you will love her adopted son Yatharva as your own. That you'll build a future with both of them — not just for love, but with responsibility."

"Go to her parents. Talk to them with respect. Arrange the wedding the way she always dreamed it. Love her the way she always wanted to be loved. Not just with flowers and gifts, but with loyalty, growth, and consistency."

Ronie paused, then added one last thing.
"And don't think it'll work the first time. If she says no, don't give up. If she ignores you, wait. If she gets angry, listen. If you have to propose in front of the world — through the media, on social platforms — do it. She still loves you. But she hated who you became. And now… if you're truly a better man, she'll come back. But not easily. Be ready for a fight. A real one."

Vihaan wiped his face. His hands trembled, but his heart was clear.

"I'll do it, Ronie. I'll do it all. This time… not to win her back, but to deserve her."

After the call ended, Vihaan sat on the edge of the footpath, his phone still in his hand, eyes staring blankly at the ground. Ronie's words echoed in his mind like an alarm that had finally woken him up.

"Don't expect a yes immediately... she still loves you, but she hated who you became."

Vihaan closed his eyes, took a deep breath, and said to himself softly, "This time, I won't rush. This time, I'll do it right."

He stood up, brushed off the dust from his jeans, and started walking — not aimlessly anymore, but with purpose. His mind began to spin ideas, thoughts forming like puzzle pieces.

"I can't just show up with flowers and say I've changed. She's beyond all that now."

"She's seen pain. She's built strength. If I want to stand beside her, I need to show her that I don't just want her — I understand her."

That was the first piece. Understanding.

He thought about writing her a letter. Handwritten, from the heart. Not a text, not an email. A real letter — something she could hold. Something that carried his apology, his transformation, his truth.

Then he thought, *what if she never reads it?*

No. I need to face her. Look into her eyes. Let her see the change, not just read it.

He imagined arranging a small dinner — not fancy, not dramatic. Something meaningful. Maybe in a place that reminded her of peace. A quiet rooftop, lights hanging low, soft music in the background — just them, no crowd, no pressure. But even that felt too soon.

He shook his head. "I can't just invite her like nothing happened."

He needed a buildup. Proof.

"First... I'll reach out to her parents. Ask for their time. Seek their blessing. Not to impress them, but because they deserve to know I respect her, and them."

"Then... I'll spend time with Yatharva. Not for show — but because I truly want to. I want to love that child like my own. I already do."

He knew if Anjali saw him care for her son without expectations, maybe her walls would soften — even slightly.

And then, when the time was right…

He would stand in front of her. No drama. No gimmicks. Just a ring, a promise, and the truest version of himself.

"Anjali," he rehearsed under his breath, "I don't deserve a second chance. But I've built myself into a man who's ready to earn one. I don't want to fix the past. I want to build a new future — with you. With Yatharva. As your partner, your support... your husband."

For a brief second, he smiled.

The first real smile in weeks.

Because now… he had a plan. Not to *get her back*. But to win her trust. Slowly. Genuinely. Deeply.

And for the first time, he wasn't scared of rejection.

He was ready to fight for her.

Notebook in hand, head full of determination, Vihaan sat on the edge of a bench near the main chowk of the city. For the first time in months, he had a clear plan. A real one. He would start by talking to her parents, then slowly become a part of Yatharva's life — not by begging, but by being present, consistent, and true.

As he closed the book and looked up, he suddenly heard the sharp honk of a siren.

He turned his head instinctively — and there it was.

Her convoy.

A line of white government cars, police jeeps at front and back, cutting through the crowd with authority and elegance. In the middle was her official vehicle — a sleek white SUV with the District Magistrate's plate.

Inside, was *her.*

Even through the tinted glass, he could sense her presence — composed, commanding, and yet gentle.

People on the road began to stop and watch.

"Woh dekho, madam aa rahi hain… IAS madam…" a shopkeeper said, standing on his toes.

"She's the one who stopped the illegal demolition near the slum last week," another added proudly.

"Bachon ke school ke liye zameen waapas li thi… bina kisi dar ke," an elderly rickshaw-puller said with folded hands, as if offering silent respect.

Vihaan's heart swelled. His chest tightened.

This… this is who she had become.

Not just someone with a powerful badge. But someone who was *using* that power to protect people who had nothing.

He stood there quietly, watching her convoy glide past, the flags fluttering, the police escort clearing the path — but her reputation had already cleared a space in people's hearts.

Just then, two men standing near him whispered something that turned his blood cold.

"Did you hear? That builder… the one whose illegal colony she shut down — he's furious."

"Yeah, I heard he's planning something dangerous… someone said he offered money to get her killed."

Vihaan froze.

“What?” he turned and asked instinctively, his voice firm.

The two men looked startled. “Haan bhai… kuch log keh rahe the kal ki madam ke khilaaf kuch bad intention wala plan ban raha hai. Woh real estate wala toh barbaad ho gaya… aur jab tak madam zinda hai, uska khel khatam hai.”

The world around him blurred for a moment.

His heart pounded.

Someone's planning to kill her?

Suddenly, everything — the letter, the proposal, the apology — all of it felt useless in comparison.

His plan wasn't just about love anymore.

It was about *protecting the woman who once protected him from himself.*

She had stood between corrupt power and innocent lives. She had fought alone when no one else had the courage. She was fearless — but that didn't mean she wasn't in danger.

And he knew one thing clearly now:
Before becoming her life partner…
He had to become her *protector.*

His fists clenched. His mind raced.

“If someone even thinks about harming her…”

No. He couldn't sit back and wait anymore.

This wasn't just about flowers and rings.

This was about standing next to her — not behind her — in a war she was silently fighting every single day.

He pulled out his phone and made a call.

“Ronie… something's wrong. There's a serious threat to Anjali. I'm not going anywhere till I make sure she's safe.”

Chapter 09: A Close Call and Closer Truths

The morning air in Anjali's home carried a strange weight.

It looked like any other peaceful day — the clatter of tea cups in the kitchen, Yatharva's giggles echoing from the living room as he played with his grandmother, and sunlight painting the walls golden.

But **Anjali's heart was far from calm.**

Anjali, dressed in a soft pastel cotton saree, had just stepped into the dining area. Her hair was still damp from the shower, her eyes slightly tired but sharp. She had a long day ahead—review meetings, a site inspection, and a public hearing scheduled. But this morning, she allowed herself a quiet breakfast with her family. She sat at the breakfast table, gently stirring her tea, her thoughts miles away. Her smile was soft for her baby, but her eyes carried a storm.

Because **she knew.**

Yesterday, when the truck came screeching close to her convoy, when her driver took that wild turn to avoid it — that wasn't just a reckless accident. No. She had felt it. *It was planned.*

But she hadn't told anyone. Not her parents, not her team.
Because she didn't want more chaos.
Because… she had just found peace after years.

"I just brought my son home. I waited for him… fought for him… prayed for him."
"Now this? Threats? Attacks? Drama?"
Her heart sank.

All she wanted was to spend time with Yatharva. Watch him grow, listen to his first words, hold him every night without the fear of being called into danger.
But being an IAS officer — and a woman who stood up to corruption — came with a price.

Her phone, however, had a different plan.

It rang. Again. And again.

The landline too. Her sister's phone. Her father's.

Calls. Texts. Missed calls.

All from familiar names—friends, colleagues, even local news reporters.

Everyone asking the same question:
"Are you okay? Were you in that convoy yesterday?"

She frowned, confused. "What happened all of a sudden? Why are all asking about her well-being suddenly?"Though in a corner of her head, she was thinking may that yesterday's issue is leaked.

Just then, the news anchor's voice blared from the living room TV, loud and urgent.

Then the news flashed on-screen.

"DM Anjali Sharma's convoy narrowly escapes a possible planned accident."

"In a shocking near-death incident, a truck lost control and almost collided with the convoy of District Magistrate Anjali Sharma. Sources claim it was more than just an accident. Thankfully, the IAS officer's vehicle narrowly escaped with a quick diversion by her escort team. Police have not confirmed foul play yet, but early reports suggest the truck was tampered with…"

And everything broke loose.

Her phone wouldn't stop ringing. Family, friends, colleagues, even old batchmates — all calling, panicked.

Her mother held her hand tightly. Her father stood in stunned silence. And Anjali just sat there, silent.

She hadn't wanted the world to know. Now, every person who loved her would carry this fear. Every moment with Yatharva would be under a cloud of tension.

Outside, just minutes later, a young man came to the gate.

"Job application," he told the guard. "For house help."

The guard informed the family, but this time, **Vihaan** stepped forward.

He had been at the house since early morning — not because he was invited, but because he couldn't stay away after what he heard.

He walked up to the gate, calm on the outside, but his senses on fire.

"What's your name?"
"Ajay, sir."
"Where have you worked before?"
"Sector 6… but the family moved out."
"Any references?"
"No… I mean, they didn't leave anything…"

Vihaan watched the man's face — too many pauses, too little clarity. His gut screamed.

"Who told you there was a vacancy here?"
"Uh… just heard from someone in the market."
"Which market? Name?"
"I—I don't remember the name…"

That was enough.

"Thank you," Vihaan said, lips tight. "We'll call you if we need you."

The guard sent the man away, and Vihaan walked straight into the house, where Anjali was still seated, now surrounded by tense silence.

He looked at her — her face still composed, her posture still upright, but her eyes… tired.

"Anjali," he said softly. "Why didn't you tell anyone?"

She looked up, surprised at his sudden presence.

"You *knew* yesterday that the truck incident wasn't random, right? And still you kept quiet?"

Her silence answered everything.

"You have to apply for more security. Get additional escort vehicles. Extra guards here. You have a child now, Anjali. You have a family to think of."

His voice cracked slightly at the end.

"I swear, I'll stay close from now on. Around the house, around your car. Whatever it takes. I'll be there."

But instead of gratitude, Anjali's eyes flared.

She stood up suddenly, the chair making a sharp sound as it slid back.

"NOW you'll be there?" Her voice was low and shaking. "NOW you care?"

Vihaan froze.

She stepped closer. "Where was all this concern when I needed it the most? When I was alone, fighting court cases, getting humiliated by society, struggling through sleepless nights waiting for the adoption to get approved?"

Her voice cracked.

"Where were you when I cried alone in hospital corridors, signed legal papers without anyone by my side, when people said I'm too ambitious to be a mother?"

Tears stung her eyes but didn't fall.

"Don't come now like some saviour. You don't get to *protect* me now. You lost that right when you *left*."

Vihaan opened his mouth to speak, but nothing came out.

"Please," she said, voice steady again. "Just leave me. Don't confuse my life now. I've rebuilt it brick by brick. I don't need another man trying to 'fix' me."

She turned away.

And that was it.

The air between them was heavy with things unsaid, moments gone, and wounds too deep.

Vihaan stood silently for a moment, his fists clenched, heart shattered — not because she shouted, but because she was right.

The house fell silent after the storm.

Everyone went back to their rooms, shaken by the news, by the near-accident, and by the raw, honest explosion that had just occurred between Anjali and Vihaan.

But **he didn't move.**
Not from the corner where he stood.
Not even an inch.

Her words were still ringing in his ears—sharp, clear, and honest.
"Where was your concern when I actually needed it?"
"Don't confuse my life now... I rebuilt it brick by brick."

She didn't scream out of hatred.
She screamed because she was hurt. Deeply. Silently. For years.

Moments passed. Maybe minutes. Maybe more.

Then came the faint sound of a car engine outside. He walked to the window just in time to see **her official vehicle leaving.**

She was on her way to the office.

Her posture was perfect, her eyes straight ahead, her face calm.
But **he knew better now.**
Behind that calm lived wounds no one had ever tried to heal.

His heart tugged, his legs moved before his mind caught up.
He rushed to the parking space, grabbed his helmet, started his old bike.

"I'm going with her," he muttered. "No matter what."

He didn't care if she didn't want him there.
He didn't care if the police convoy would wave him off.
He just knew — **she was in danger. And he had to be nearby.**

The DM's convoy was just ahead as he pulled out into the road. He followed at a safe distance. Not too close. Not too far. Just enough to watch over her, even silently.

The wind brushed past his face, but his mind wasn't on the road — it was in the past.

"She gave me everything back then... her time, her trust, her loyalty."

"And I gave her... distance, excuses, silence."

His jaw tightened.

"I was egoistic. I didn't know how to handle someone so pure, so powerful."

"She deserved love... not lessons. And I became the biggest one."

He kept riding, the convoy in sight, but his thoughts far heavier than the engine beneath him.

"She's not going to forgive me easily."

"Maybe not ever."

"But this isn't about getting her back anymore. It's about showing her she's not alone — not now, not ever again."

He stopped at a red light for a moment and watched her car from afar.
The flags fluttered. The tinted glass shielded her expression.
But he could still feel her presence — guarded, distant… but strong.

And broken.

Not because she was weak.
But because no one ever stayed long enough to hold her when she fell.

And now, he knew what he had to do.

Not rush her.
Not win her.
Not demand her love back.

Just wait.
Wait patiently.

And in the meantime—heal what the world and *he* had broken.
One small step at a time.
From a distance, if he had to.
Silently, if that's what it takes.

The sun had climbed high by the time Anjali's convoy reached the district office.

As the doors opened, the staff rose from their desks, the security team stood straighter, and citizens waiting outside leaned forward with quiet admiration. The crowd whispered her name with respect, like she was more than an officer — like she was hope.

She stepped out in her crisp beige saree, sunglasses hiding the tiredness in her eyes, her every step calm, measured, confident.

But inside?

She was anything but calm.

The news report. The truck incident. The silence she had chosen. The child she had just brought home. The fear in her mother's eyes that morning.
It was all too much — but she had no choice. **She had to wear strength like skin.**

"Madam, MLA sir is waiting in the conference room," her assistant said as she entered.

She nodded, pushed the thoughts aside, and walked in.

The day unfolded like every other.
Meetings. Public complaints. File approvals. Site visit briefings.

But somewhere in between…

Anjali felt a lump in her throat.

"I didn't become an officer to feel this helpless."
"I've fought for everyone. But now I want to fight for myself too."
"I just got my son... all I want is time with him. Peace."

And yet, peace was the last thing the world was offering.

She pressed her fingers against her forehead as the staff left the room.

Alone, for just a second, she allowed herself to drop the mask.

She closed her eyes, her voice whispering in her own head — *"Why now?"*

Outside, the convoy vehicles remained parked as the security stayed alert.

A few metres away, across the road near a tea stall, **Vihaan sat on his bike**, helmet on, pretending to scroll through his phone. But his eyes? Fixed on the gate. Watching. Waiting.

He saw her enter earlier. Saw her walk tall as always.

But he also saw something else.

Two men had been standing near the gate for over twenty minutes now.

Not talking. Not moving.

One kept adjusting his cap nervously, the other pretended to look at a newspaper but didn't flip the page once. They weren't there for public service — that much he could bet.

Vihaan's breath slowed. His eyes narrowed.

He got off the bike and began walking casually toward them, blending in with the small crowd that hovered near the office.

One of the men noticed him and turned away.

The other lowered the newspaper and slowly walked to the edge of the street.

Too smooth.
Too careful.

Vihaan pulled out his phone and dialed to his friend at the police station

“Two unknowns outside Anjali’s office. Suspicious behavior. Can you send someone from the local police team she trusts? Discreetly.”

The officer responded instantly, “Already on it. Don’t confront them. Just watch.”

Vihaan’s eyes didn’t blink.

“I don’t care if she hates me. I don’t care if she never forgives me. But if someone tries to harm her now…”

“They’ll have to go through me first.”

Chapter 10: Truth in the Shadow of Explosions

Days had passed since the two suspects outside Anjali's office were arrested.

But no name. No connection.
No clue who was actually pulling the strings behind the scenes.

Anjali remained calm on the surface — her posture always perfect, her eyes sharp — but inside, she was unsettled. Not by fear… but by the silence of the threat.

Someone wanted her gone. Someone powerful enough to stay hidden.

And in the background of it all… **Vihaan never left.**

He never entered her world again, not directly — but quietly, he stayed close.
He followed her convoys, watched the gates of her office, chased the shadows she couldn't see.

And slowly, one by one, **he began catching them.**
Men loitering with hidden cameras. A guy pretending to be a vendor near her bungalow.
Each time, Vihaan noticed them, chased them, **and helped get them arrested.**

No recognition. No thanks.
Just one silent mission: *Protect her.*

That Sunday, Anjali had been invited to **inaugurate the National Trade & Cultural Fair**. Dressed in an elegant yet simple cotton silk saree, she carried her power with grace. The media was waiting. The public stood in long queues.

The event went smoothly. Applause. Speeches. Smiles.

But as she stepped out of the main pavilion toward her car, **something caught her eye.**

In the parking area, near the exit, **a man was pinned to the ground by someone.**

Anjali stepped closer.
It was **Vihaan** — gripping a man by his collar, yelling.

"Tell me who sent you! Who's behind all these attacks? Who are you working for?"

The man was bruised, trying to reach into his pocket.

Anjali's eyes narrowed.
She rushed forward.
The moment she saw the man's hand — she froze.

He had a bomb trigger in his grip.

Without thinking, Anjali shouted, "Stop! Move back!"

The police tackled the man before he could press anything. The device was snatched from his hand. Chaos followed.

The crowd screamed. The media turned. Police pulled up barricades.

And amid that chaos, **Anjali walked up to Vihaan**. Her eyes didn't hold thanks.

They held rage.

"Why are you doing all this?" she asked coldly.

He opened his mouth, breathless, trying to explain.

But she cut him off.

"Instead of taking your help, I would prefer dying alone — in any of these so-called accidents. At least I would die with peace."

The words hit like stones.
But she wasn't done.

“I know you’ve been following my convoy for weeks. One of my officers told me. You think I didn’t notice?”

She stepped closer. Her voice got lower, sharper.

“You’ve become the gossip of my department. People say I have a lover now — ‘DM madam’s ex is stalking her again.’”

She smirked — coldly.

“Let them talk. I don’t care about your love. You had your chance. You blew it. I don’t want you around. Not as a man. Not as a protector. Not even as a shadow.”

She turned to leave.

The crowd was silent now. The suspect had been taken away. Media flashed lights. Security shouted instructions.

And **Vihaan stood still**, saying nothing.

Because… what could he say?

He had broken her once.

Now, no effort seemed enough to earn even her **belief.**

But just as she was about to enter her car, **one of her senior officers walked up quietly.**

“Ma’am,” he said gently, “I don’t know what happened between you two in the past, and I won’t interfere in personal matters…”

She turned to him, raising an eyebrow.

He continued, “But what I do know is — he’s been helping us. Since the day you asked him to leave, he hasn’t gone home. He’s been living in a small rented room near the collectorate, barely sleeping, working on every suspicious activity around your office. Most of the arrests we’ve made recently — ma’am, it’s because of his tip-offs.”

Anjali blinked. Slowly.

"He's been part of our internal investigation quietly. He doesn't want credit. He just… wants you safe."

The officer paused, then added with quiet honesty —
"Whatever his mistakes were before, ma'am… now? He's more sincere than most of us combined."

Anjali didn't reply.

She sat in the car, eyes forward, heart caught between rage and realisation.

She didn't know what hurt more — the past he left her with…
Or the present he was silently saving for her.

Chapter 11: Scars Behind the Smile (Extended)

The road home was familiar, yet Anjali felt like she was being driven into her past.

She sat silently in the back seat, her saree still neat, her hair still pinned perfectly, her public face still intact — but inside, something had cracked. Not from the incident. Not from the bomb.
From the way her heart reacted — *for a second* — when she saw **him**.

Vihaan.

There he was again, putting himself in danger, trying to protect her like some dramatic savior in a film.
And for a brief moment, just for a fleeting second, her heart whispered:
"Maybe... maybe he really has changed."

But before that thought could settle, it was drowned by the scream of old memories.
Memories she didn't want… but could never forget.

Flashback

She remembered the day she sat on his family's sofa, trying to explain herself — calm, composed, hoping to be heard.

But all she received was suspicion.
Judgement.
Mockery.

"You talk too much," said one of his aunts.
"You roam in offices full of men — what will you do in our house?" another spat.
And then the worst —
"Girls like you don't become good wives. You become problems."

She looked at Vihaan, silently pleading for him to speak.
To say *something — anything.*

But he just stood there.

"You're wrong, Anjali," he had said finally.
Those words hurt more than anything his family had said.

She tried to defend herself. Tried to say she was not wrong. That she had always been honest.

That's when it happened.

One of his relatives stood up and **slapped her** across the face.

A deafening silence followed.

And Vihaan? He didn't even flinch.

She stormed out that day, her hands shaking, her chest burning.

But that wasn't the end.

Every time they fought after that — he got crueler.
Once, at the railway station, he accused her of using him.
Once, outside her coaching center, he called her "fake."
And when she broke down and said she couldn't take the pressure, said she didn't want to live — he had simply scoffed.

"It's all drama, Anjali. I'm done with your emotional tricks."

She had fallen to her knees. Begged him. Cried on roads. Messaged. Called.

Nothing.

And eventually… her body gave up.
She was hospitalised. Her weight dropped.
She didn't eat properly for weeks.
Her soul had shattered in silence.

But no one ever saw that side of her.
Because she stood back up.

Wiped her tears.
And became **Anjali Sharma, IAS.**

Present

That was the Anjali now staring out of the car window, thinking — *"How dare he come back and pretend like it never happened?"*

She hated herself for that moment of weakness at the fair — the way her heart skipped when she saw him trying to save her.

"Where was this version of him when I needed saving from his words?"

The car slowed near her home.

"Ma'am?" the driver asked gently. "We've reached."

No answer.

"Ma'am?"

Still nothing.

He stopped the car, got out, walked to her door, and opened it softly.

"Ma'am," he said again, his voice kind, "all okay?"

She looked at him, lost in the weight of her own silence.

"I know it's not my place," he continued, "but… I've seen you make bold decisions. You've never been wrong, Ma'am. If this one doesn't feel right… don't force it. Some people deserve to be left behind."

She blinked — once.
Then smiled.
It was weak, but genuine.

"Thank you," she said quietly.

And stepped out.

Inside the House

The scent of sandalwood lingered in the hall. Her father was sitting in the drawing room, reading a newspaper. He looked up immediately.

"You okay, beta?"

She nodded, unconvincing. "I just… needed to talk."

They sat down. Moments later, her uncle joined too.

She didn't rant. She didn't cry. She spoke plainly.

"He's still trying. Protecting me. Saving me. But I don't know if I should feel anything anymore. He broke me once. I'm afraid if I trust him again, I won't survive a second fall."

Her father held her hand.

"Anjali, sometimes life brings back people — not to give them another chance, but to show us how far we've come without them."

Her uncle added, "Whatever you do, let it come from your strength, not your sympathy. And never… ever compromise your self-respect."

She nodded slowly. That was the reminder she needed.

After a long, warm shower, she changed into a soft cotton kurta and came downstairs.
She felt lighter. Not healed — but clear.

Dinner was being prepared. As she walked to the kitchen, she paused for a second.

Then she turned to the helper and said, "Call Vihaan."

The staff looked at her in surprise.

"Ask him to join us for dinner. And tell him… he can stay in the guest room until he decides to leave the district."

"Ma'am?" the helper asked softly, almost in shock.

She didn't smile this time.

She simply said, "This is not love. This is gratitude."

Meanwhile – At Vihaan's Rented Room

The light flickered in the small room. A fan creaked overhead. A single mat on the floor. One steel thali with untouched roti on the table.

Vihaan sat hunched, elbows on knees, staring at the cracked floor.

His mind was spiraling. **He saw every memory like a cruel movie reel.**

Anjali being humiliated.
That slap echoing through the room.
His silence.
Her tears.
His selfishness.
Her slow breakdown.

"I ruined her," he whispered.
"I destroyed the one person who ever stood by me."

The guilt was unbearable.

He had tried to fix it now — helped her, protected her, arrested those behind the threats — but none of it felt enough.

"She doesn't owe me anything. Not even this breath I'm taking."

He buried his face in his hands, feeling smaller than ever before.

A knock came at the door.

He didn't move.

Another knock.

"Sir?" a familiar voice said. "It's me… the driver."

Vihaan opened the door slowly, eyes red.

"She sent me," the driver said gently.

"For what?"

"To take you home."

Vihaan blinked. "What? Why?"

"She said — and I quote — 'He doesn't need to stay in that old room anymore. He can come back to the guest room. It's not love. It's gratitude. That's all.'"

Vihaan's breath hitched.

He shook his head. "She… she really said that?"

The driver nodded. "Yes. And sir — everyone's waiting for dinner. She asked me to bring you back *now.*"

Vihaan stood frozen for a second.

And then, almost as if the guilt had cracked open a space for humility, he slowly began to pack the few things he had — a file, a couple of shirts, his wallet, a pen she had once gifted him during their better days.

The driver watched quietly, understanding everything without asking a word.

Back at Anjali's Mansion

The porch lights were warm when the car pulled in.

No one came out to greet him.

And that was okay.

Because this wasn't a celebration. It wasn't a return.

It was a silent agreement:
You don't deserve forgiveness. But you'll get shelter.
You don't get love. But you'll be allowed to make things right. Quietly.

He stepped out of the car.

Anjali wasn't at the door.
She didn't need to be.

He walked in slowly, the air of the house familiar and heavy.
The staff offered a quiet nod.
Yatharva was upstairs, giggling in his sleep.
And at the dinner table… food had been warmed again.

And even though no one said it out loud, one thing was clear —

He wasn't forgiven.
But he wasn't unwelcome anymore.

Later all had dinner with some cold reactions and normal discussions.

Chapter 12: The Wound, the Word, the War Within

Dinner ended without drama, but the silence at the table was louder than ever.

Plates were cleared, conversations kept light, and everyone tried their best to make things look normal. But **nothing was normal**.

Especially for **Anjali**.

She had barely spoken during the meal. She avoided looking at Vihaan. She nodded when spoken to, smiled when expected — but her fingers kept curling into her palm under the table, digging deep. **Trying to hold in everything she couldn't scream.**

Her mother, in an effort to create a sense of warmth again, began asking Vihaan simple, polite questions.

"So beta, how have you been keeping? Work? Your health? The family?"

Vihaan responded kindly, with his usual soft tone. "Health is better now, Aunty. Family… I haven't seen them in months. Honestly, I'm not looking back there anymore."

Anjali's throat tightened.

Because once upon a time, *she* had begged him to cut ties with that same family — the people who had humiliated her, hit her, questioned her dignity — and he had chosen **them**.

And now, suddenly, he claimed he had let them go.

She clenched her jaw.

Anjali's father noticed the stiffness in her eyes. Her uncle saw the tension growing in her shoulders. They quickly diverted the conversation.

"Well," her father said, chuckling gently, "since Anjali is not on fast today, let's eat before she walks out on all of us again."

Everyone chuckled lightly.

Anjali smiled — barely.

Dinner resumed. Her sisters joined in. Yatharva babbled in his high chair, stealing bits of attention from everyone.

And for the first time in many weeks, **the family ate together. Fully. With some laughter. With some awkward pauses. But with food on every plate.**

Later That Night – Tea Gathering

It was 10:30 PM when they all gathered again in the living room for chai.

There was a cozy familiarity to this — floor cushions, soft lights, the clink of cups, and the smell of elaichi in every sip.

Anjali sat cross-legged beside her youngest sister. Vihaan sat quietly, careful not to sit too close, or make anyone uncomfortable. He simply sipped his tea in silence.

But her sister noticed something.

"Bhaiya… your hand. What happened?" she asked, pointing to the torn sleeve.

Everyone looked at him. Anjali included.

"It's nothing," he said, trying to hide the wound. "Just a small cut."

Her father asked gently, "How?"

Vihaan hesitated, then answered softly. "It happened during that encounter with the bomb suspect… the one who tried to attack the convoy. During the scuffle, I got scratched, that's all."

Anjali froze.

Because **she had been in that convoy.**

She remembered that moment — the sudden jolt, the screams of officers, the chaos… and later being told the man had been subdued.

She looked at his hand.

Then straight into his eyes.

And then… her voice exploded.

"WHO asked you to play hero?!"

Everyone flinched. Even the house help paused mid-step.

Anjali stood, her tone rising like a storm.

"Are you all in a race now? Want a bravery medal? A newspaper headline? 'Ex-boyfriend saves IAS officer' — is that the story you want to sell?"

Vihaan didn't respond.

Anjali's voice cracked — but she didn't let it show as emotion. She turned it into rage.

"Don't expect anything from me. Not forgiveness, not gratitude. I'm the worst person alive, right? I push people away. I cut off love. I protect myself. So don't come here acting like a saviour."

The room was dead silent.

She turned to the maid.

"Do his dressing and clean up. I'm going to spend time with Yatharva. I need him. Not this circus."

And just like that, **she left.**

The Breakdown That Followed

After she left, **Vihaan sat frozen.** His hand trembled now — not from pain, but shame.

Her words had cracked him open.
Not because she insulted him.
But because she was still bleeding… and she was right.

He had tried to help her from the outside — but he never showed up when she had begged for him at her lowest.

And now she was punishing herself for ever needing him again.

Her mother walked over, quietly sat beside him, and placed her hand on his shoulder.

She looked at him — his face pale, his eyes red, barely able to hold his composure.

And she said softly, **"She doesn't hate you."**

He looked up, confused, teary.

Her mother continued, "She's hurt. Deeply. She still keeps your pictures, you know? I've seen them. In her phone. She hides the screen every time I walk in. But I've seen them."

Vihaan looked down, completely broken now.

"She loved you, beta. And you broke her spirit. You never stood up for her. Never held her when she fell. And now… she doesn't know how to ask for love again."

He nodded, silently crying.

"Don't try to win her. **Heal her.** Fix what you shattered. And if you can't do that — leave. Don't stay halfway and destroy her again."

He whispered, voice shaking: **"I won't leave this time. Not until I fix it all. But first… I need to catch the man who tried to kill her."**

Her mother smiled. "Then start there."

The Call That Changed Everything

Just as the house went quiet again and most had gone to their rooms, **Vihaan's phone buzzed**.

A call.

He answered.

The voice on the other side was calm but cautious.

"Your suspicion was right," the man said. "The person behind the bomb plan, the surveillance, the threats — it's that same real estate giant. The one Madam shut down for illegal land grabbing."

Vihaan's jaw tightened.

"I have everything," the man said. "Proof. Emails. Voice recordings. CCTV footage. But don't ever mention my name. Please."

"You have my word," Vihaan said, heart pounding.

He immediately called the police inspector he trusted and forwarded the entire file.

Then he contacted the court's clerk directly.

Within an hour, he had a confirmation.

The real estate mogul was being arrested the next morning. No chance of bail. No escape.

A Quiet Celebration

He walked back to the hall, where only **Anjali's mother** remained, sipping tea in silence.

He sat down slowly beside her.

"We got him," he said, voice thick with emotion. "The one behind the threats. He's going to jail. This is over."

She looked at him — and for the first time — smiled with pride.

"Good," she said, pouring him another cup. "Then let's have one more chai."

And so they did.

No music.
No clapping.
Just two people sitting in a silent room, sharing the warmth of justice — and the long road ahead that would now finally begin to feel possible.

Chapter 13: The Morning She Didn't See Coming

The morning light slipped softly through the curtains of Anjali's room.

She had barely slept.

The weight of her outburst the night before still lingered on her chest. She wasn't ashamed — but she was exhausted.

She looked at the clock. **6:40 AM.**

Yatharva was still asleep beside her, his tiny fist tucked under his cheek, breathing soft and steady. She stroked his hair gently, whispering:

"Tum hi ho meri shanti, mere liye sabse safe jagah."

She kissed his forehead and quietly got up, slipping on her shawl, tying her hair into a loose bun. It was still too early to start work — but her routine never waited.

She stepped out onto the balcony, holding a warm cup of adrak wali chai.

The breeze was cool, the trees still silent, and the air smelled of wet earth.

But her mind? **Storming.**

The words she'd shouted at Vihaan last night kept echoing.
Her voice, her pain — all of it still raw, fresh, open.

And yet, beneath the anger, **something had cracked open.**

He caught the bomber. He bled to protect me. And yet... he never asked for credit.
He never even raised his voice when I shouted. He just sat there and took it.
Not like before...

She shut her eyes tight.

"No, Anjali. Don't go there."

She wasn't ready to hope again.

Downstairs, the staff had begun their day. Anjali's mother was already in the kitchen, instructing the cook softly.

Suddenly, the front gate bell rang.

One of the officers from the District Police Headquarters stood outside, holding an official sealed file.

The house help took it, signed the paper, and brought it inside.

"Ma'am… DM ma'am ke liye urgent file aayi hai,(Ma'am There's a file for DM ma'am)" he said to her mother.

Anjali came down just in time to see it being placed on the table.

Her mother handed it to her. "Dekho toh sahi…"(Check it once)

Anjali opened the file. Page one was a court-stamped report.

Her eyes ran across the text.

Then widened.

**"The real estate developer arrested this morning.
Charged with criminal conspiracy, attempted murder, bribery, and obstruction of a government officer."**

Her breath caught.

It was him.

The same man she had stood against.
The same one who had sent goons, planted fear, and threatened her safety for weeks.

She flipped to the next page. Evidence summary.
CCTV visuals. Audio call records. Bank transfer logs.

And at the bottom…

"Key intelligence sourced through unofficial but credible field inputs."

She didn't need to ask who it was.

Vihaan.

Her fingers froze on the page.

Her mother, watching her silently, placed a hand on her shoulder.

"He did it, Anjali. Quietly. Without needing to prove anything. He just wanted you safe."

Anjali didn't answer. She stared at the document.

Her voice, when it came, was barely above a whisper.

"He found the man. He really did it."

Her mother nodded. "And he shared the news with me last night. But he didn't come to you. He said, 'She deserves to hear it officially, not from me.'"

Anjali's throat tightened.

He didn't rush in. He didn't gloat. He didn't use it as a chance to win me over. He just... stood at a distance, and did the right thing.

She closed the file and quietly walked back to the balcony, holding her tea with both hands.

The city outside was waking up.

But something in her heart was already shifting.

She wasn't ready to forgive.
Not ready to forget.
But maybe… just maybe… she was ready to admit something had changed.

And maybe the man she once loved was trying, for the first time, to love her right — by asking for nothing at all.

The city was still gently yawning into its morning routine, but **Anjali** had been wide awake since dawn.

The weight of the court file from the previous day — the one confirming the arrest of the man who tried to end her life — still sat untouched on the side table. Justice was served. Peace, on paper, had been restored.

But her mind was anything but peaceful.

She stood on the balcony with a lukewarm cup of tea in her hand, watching the world move slowly beneath her. The breeze was soft. Leaves rustled. The scent of wet earth rose from last night's brief drizzle.

And then… she saw **him**.

Vihan.

There, in the small park across the street — barefoot on the grass, the morning sun pouring onto his shoulders — he was doing **Surya Namaskar**.

His arms moved in flow, his spine rising and bending in rhythm with the breath. Calm. Grounded. Sincere.

But what caught her eye — what stopped her heart for a second — wasn't the yoga.

It was **the kurta**.

White. Crisp. Plain. The exact style she had once told him she liked. No fancy prints. No gym tanks. Just *simplicity*.

And then… **she smiled.**

A tiny one. Soft. Real.
The kind of smile that slips out before you remember why you stopped smiling in the first place.

For a second, her heart forgot the pain.
Forgot the slap.
The betrayal.
The silence.
It just saw him — **trying.**

But then **he looked up**.

Their eyes met.

And that's when she remembered everything.
The hurt.
The distance.
The wall she'd built so carefully around herself.

She instantly turned her face away — toward the skyline — as if the clouds were suddenly more interesting.

But her chest was rising quicker now.
And her hands… slightly trembling.

Down below, **Vihan paused**, frozen in the last posture.

He didn't call out.
He didn't wave.

He just watched her turn away, a small smile tugging at the corner of his lips.

Because that brief moment — that split-second smile she couldn't hide — had just told him more than any word could.

She hadn't forgotten how to feel.

He closed his eyes. Folded his hands. Finished the asana.

And whispered to himself:

**"That was her heart peeking through.
One day… she won't look away."**

Chapter 14: Pyaar Ka Live Telecast

The morning began like any other — chai being served at the desk, piles of files awaiting signatures, and Anjali seated in her cabin, typing a note with clinical precision.

"Madam, ek minute..." her PA said, slightly too excited.

She looked up.

The wall-mounted TV in the staff bay just outside her office was playing **a live news channel**, and the anchor's voice was buzzing with admiration.

Her staff had gathered around the screen, whispering and smiling like schoolkids watching a romantic scene unfold.

She sighed. "Kya chal raha hai?"

Her PA smiled. "Madam, Vihan sir ka live interview aa raha hai. News channel pe! He's being praised for his role in catching the real estate mafia man."

Anjali raised her eyebrows slightly but didn't react.
She leaned back in her chair, crossed her arms, and let the audio play in the background —*just to be aware*, not to engage.
Or so she told herself.

On the TV Screen

The camera zoomed in on **Vihan**, seated in a clean pastel shirt, hair slightly ruffled, and eyes full of calm. The anchor beside him was smiling wide.

Anchor: "Mr. Vihan, congratulations! You've earned a lot of praise recently — unofficially helping in a highly sensitive district-level investigation, remaining discreet, and doing your work without media buzz. People are calling you the unsung hero of the DM's security!"

Vihan gave a polite smile. “Thank you. But honestly, I didn’t do it for recognition. I just… did what was right.”

Anchor: “You’ve proven yourself smart, calm, physically fit, emotionally stable, and well-spoken... also, let’s not ignore this — **you’re extremely good-looking!**” *[she laughs teasingly]* “So, tell the nation — why is someone like you still single?”

Vihan smiled slowly. His eyes softened. His voice lowered just a little.

And then he answered:

“Mujhe Prem, Pyaar, Ishq, Mohabbat sab hua. Aur jab hua… tab se bas usi ka hoke reh gaya.”

“Wo naraz hai… khafa hai mujhse. Aur uska gussa jaayaz hai. Maine zindagi mein bohot galtiyan ki hain.”
“Lekin mujhe yakeen hai… paschatap ke baad daaman kabhi khali nahi gaya.”

The anchor blinked — surprised at the depth in his answer.

He continued, his voice just a touch more emotional now.

“Woh bohot narm dil hai. Samjhdaar hai. Aur sach kahoon toh, mere jaisa insaan shayad uske layak kabhi tha hi nahi.”
“Lekin aaj bhi… har subah usi ke naam se shuru hoti hai. Har raat uski yaadon mein khatam.”

And then, looking directly into the camera, his voice trembling just slightly:

“Agar tum dekh rahi ho toh… bas itna kehna tha — I love you.”
“Tum meri zindagi ho.”
“Aur main roz tumse thoda aur zyada pyaar karta hoon.”

The entire newsroom went silent. Even the anchor had no follow-up question for a moment.

Back at Anjali's Office

There was a pin-drop silence in the office corridor.

Every staff member who had teased her secretly about "DM ma'am's mystery man" now stood stunned — faces turned towards her cabin window.

Inside, **Anjali sat frozen.**

Her hand still rested near the pen. The file in front of her remained unsigned.

She had heard every word.

She felt her throat tighten, her heart… betray her once again.

Not because she wanted to forgive.
Not because she wanted to melt.

But because that man — the one who once broke her into pieces — was now showing the world how deeply he loved her… *without asking for anything in return.*

And he wasn't trying to fix the past.

He was just… confessing.

Not to her privately.

But **to the world.**

Her fingers lightly tapped the desk. Her eyes refused to meet anyone else's.

Her PA peeked in carefully. "Ma'am, should I mute the TV?"

Anjali didn't speak.

She just nodded once.

And as the sound faded, she whispered under her breath, so softly only she could hear it:

"Stupid man…"

Then she turned back to her file.

But the curve in her lips — however brief — had already been noticed by every eye outside the glass door.

The moment the interview ended, and the news anchor smiled back into the camera, the office returned to motion — staff murmured excitedly, cups of chai clinked again, and papers started shuffling.

But inside her cabin, **Anjali was completely still.**

Her phone, lying face-down on the desk, vibrated once. Then again. Then again.
And then it *rang*. Loud. Persistently.

She sighed and flipped it over.

Caller ID: Mitali (College Bestie)
Before she could think — she answered.

"Hello?"

"BHAIII... TU KYA LUCKY HAI YAAR!
Just saw the clip! I was in a meeting — and my colleague showed me your ex on national TV confessing his love like some SRK-Devdas combo!"

Anjali rolled her eyes, already regretting the call. "Mita, please don't—"

"No no no, don't even 'please' me.
He said *I love you* on a national platform, Anjali. People don't say that even in private these days!"

Anjali walked to the window, rubbing her forehead, still in denial of the circus unfolding.

"And let's talk about that kurta look. Bro. This man is working out, doing yoga, saving districts, solving crimes, looking like a poetry book in motion. Tu usse naraz thi toh theek hai, but now what? He's literally apologising with his life!"

Anjali pressed her lips together, staring at the sky.

"Mita, he… hurt me. Deeply. You know that."

"I do. And I'll never forget what he did to you. But you also told me once…"

"If he ever *becomes* the man I needed, maybe I'll look at him again."

"Well guess what, Aanj. He didn't just become that man. He became *more.*"

Just then, **another call beeped in — this time, from Shikha**, her UPSC batchmate.

Anjali didn't pick it up.

Another WhatsApp ping.

Then another.

Then one from **her school friend group** —
"Kya baat hai madam, DM sahiba ke liye live proposal ho raha hai? Kya jawab diya?"
"Shaadi kab hai? Venue toh mujhe fix karne dena please."
"Arre tu toh national crush nikli!"

She sat down again, phone in hand, overwhelmed.

A part of her wanted to scream.
Another part… wanted to smile and cry at the same time.

Because **after years of silence**, people were finally saying her name in the context of love again — not pain.

But her heart still throbbed with a thousand questions.

Yes, he had changed.
Yes, his eyes looked sincere.
Yes, he didn't demand love… only expressed it.

But what if he failed her again?

"Kya ek baar todne wale ko dobara bharosa diya jaa sakta hai?"
Can a person who once broke you... ever be trusted again?

Her phone buzzed again.

This time, **Mitali sent a voice note.**

"I know you're mad. But stop punishing your own heart now, yaar. You said you wanted truth, growth, and sincerity. He's giving you all three — on a silver platter.
Just… think about it. You don't have to forgive him. But maybe… stop hiding from how much this meant to you."

She played the voice note twice.

Then locked her phone.
And sighed — long, deep, silent.

She wasn't ready to reply.
But **she wasn't untouched either.**

Chapter 15: A House Full of Whispers, A Heart Full of Thunder

Back at the district office, the excitement from Vihan's interview hadn't faded — not even by afternoon.

Anjali sat at her desk, trying to focus, but the entire staff outside her cabin was busy discussing the same thing.

Him.

One of the young female staffers whispered to her colleague, just loud enough to reach Anjali's ears:

"Ma'am, kya lagta hai... kaun hogi woh lucky girl jiske liye sir itna bol gaye?"

"Jo bhi hogi... kismat wali hai yaar," said another.

Another giggled. **"Main hoti toh kab ka haan kar deti. Live TV pe propose karna koi mazak hai?"**

Then came the sassy one:
"Waise… didn't he see our Madam? Beautiful, powerful, famous — and still single. He could've proposed her! Why is he stuck on someone else?"

A quieter one added seriously,
"Mujhe toh lagta hai… woh Madam hi thi. Sir yahin toh ruk kar reh rahe hain. Har mushkil mein unke saath. Madam ne kabhi khud nahi bataya ki woh single kyun hain…"

From inside her cabin, **Anjali heard everything.**

She sipped her coffee slowly.

A small, involuntary smile tugged at her lips.

But she didn't say a word.

She just closed the file in front of her, got up gracefully, picked up her bag, and left the office — leaving behind a flurry of guessing games and rising curiosity.

At Home: A Surprise Brewing

As Anjali stepped into her house, she was hit by a blast of **sweet, spicy, and festive aromas.**

Gajar ka halwa, poori, kachauri, fried dry fruits, kesar chai, and even fresh mogra flowers tied at the entrance. The house was alive — buzzing with activity.

The kitchen was full. Her sisters were running with plates. The house help was decorating the backyard. Her mother was shouting instructions.

But no one greeted her.

No one even noticed she'd come in.

She stood still, stunned.

"Wait... what's happening?"

She climbed up, changed into something more comfortable, and came back down, slightly amused and slightly suspicious.

"**Maa!**" she called out finally.
"What's happening? Tumhara birthday toh nahi hai…? Shaadi ki anniversary? Tauji ki koi pooja? Yatharva ka kuch plan hai kya? Sab log itne busy kyun hain?!"

Her mother turned calmly, handed her a glass of water.

"Shaant ho jao, DM Madam."

Anjali gave her a confused look.

Her mom smiled, sat her down.

"Tumne Vihan ka interview dekha na?"

Anjali blinked. "Haan, toh?"

Her mother said warmly, **"Toh beta, woh hamara beta bhi hai. Aaj uska din hai. Woh issi ghar mein rehta hai. Toh uski jeet hamari jeet hai. Aur jab ghar ka beta kuch acha kare, toh ghar sajta hai, nahi?"**

Anjali sipped the water, stunned.

Her mom continued, **"Main yeh nahi keh rahi ki tum usse turant maaf karo. But usne tumhare liye itna kuch kiya hai… tumhara farz banta hai uske liye ek baar ready hona. Aaj sirf ek celebration hai — acceptance nahi."**

"Toh jao, get ready. Help bhi karo. Aur haan… acchi lagni chahiye."

Anjali couldn't argue.

So she stood up. And went to her room.

Meanwhile… Vihan Arrives

Vihan entered the house, a little surprised at the vibrant energy, the food, the laughter echoing from the kitchen.

He was welcomed with loud claps from Anjali's sisters, hugs from her chacha and chachi, and the warmest smile from her mom.

He bowed politely, **"Namaste, aunty."**

Her father patted his back proudly, and Yatharva — from the sofa — called out "*Vi-haan!*" in his tiny voice.

Vihan smiled wide, blew him a kiss, and asked softly, **"Maa... Anjali?"**

Her mom chuckled.
"Relax, beta. Don't panic so fast. Tum ab sahi raaste pe ho."

He smiled nervously.

Then she handed him a neatly folded **white kurta with pastel embroidery**.

"Woh tumhare bed pe padha tha, main laayi hoon. Change kar lo. Aaj ka star toh tum ho."

Vihan took the kurta, nodded, and went in to get ready.

And Then… She Walked In

The food was being laid out.

People were laughing. The help was lighting diyas at the mandir.

Vihan stepped out, dressed in his white kurta, clean and confident.

But then came the moment that **stopped everything.**

One of Anjali's sisters screamed:

"UFFF! Aaj toh kisi ka qatl hone wala hai bhai!"

Another one gasped loudly:

"Jhaansi ki Rani turned into Kamdev ki patni!"

The house help dropped a spoon and clutched her heart jokingly,

"Didi aaj toh nazar na lag jaaye. Aise roz sundar kyu nahi hoti aap?!"

Anjali walked down.

Wearing a **deep wine-colored saree**, her hair open in soft curls, tiny jhumkas swinging gently, eyes lined with kohl, not for charm, but for strength.

She looked like grace in motion.
Bold, calm, elegant.
And yet, **unintentionally breathtaking.**

Vihan stood **speechless.**

Mouth slightly open.

Eyes locked.

Even his breath forgot how to function for a second.

She didn't look at him directly — but she knew. She felt it.

His gaze. His admiration. His silence.

And in that moment, **she didn't smile.**
But she didn't walk away either.

She walked slowly to the mandir, placed a diya, closed her eyes, and whispered a prayer.

Not for him.

Not for love.

But maybe… for courage.

The celebration was in full swing.

Laughter echoed through the house. Plates clinked. The smell of **desi ghee**, crispy pooris, spicy dum aloo, and cardamom-laced halwa filled the air.

Everyone was seated, ready to eat.

Except Anjali.

She was still arranging bowls of pickles, telling the helpers to reduce oil in the sabzi, adjusting the salt.

Glowing. Effortlessly.

Her **saree hugged her frame just right**, her earrings danced every time she turned, and her no-nonsense DM-wali authority had, for once, taken a back seat.

She wasn't trying to impress.

But she was unintentionally destroying every man's peace in the room — especially one man's.

Before sitting down, **her mother walked up to her silently**. Smiling, she dipped her finger in black kajal and put a small **kala tikka (black dot)** behind Anjali's right ear.

"Nazar na lage meri rani ko," she whispered.
(*"Let no evil eye touch my queen."*)

Anjali rolled her eyes, blushing just a little. "Maa…"

Her mother turned dramatically toward everyone, hands on hips.

"Ab bas! Khaane pe dhyaan do sab log. Bahut ho gaya romance-shomance."
(*"Enough now! Focus on your food, not the romance going on here!"*)

Everyone laughed. Except Vihan.
He was too busy **trying to stay alive**.

Because across the table sat **Anjali**.
And **she was lethal tonight**.

He had tried everything — meditation, breathing, even chanting "Ram-Ram" in his head.
But nothing helped.

Because every time she laughed with her sister — he melted.
Every time her bangles clinked — he forgot what hunger even meant.

And then…

Vihan smiled, lifted Yetherva up, and placed the little prince in his lap.

Then, in the middle of the chaos, as everyone was distracted passing bowls and pouring chutneys, **Vihan leaned close to Yatharva's ear and whispered:**

"Bro, your mom's killing me today."

Yatharva giggled, not understanding a word, happily munching on a poori.

Vihan continued, voice low, lips barely moving:

“Grow up fast, okay? Because your future girlfriend is gonna face the toughest competition of her life.”

“Your mom… bro, she’s so—”

He paused.

Swallowed hard.

“Okay, can’t say that word in front of you.”

“But I’m dying here, yaar. I just want to hug her once.”

Yatharva dropped a tiny bit of halwa on his kurta. Vihan laughed and wiped it, continuing:

“You know my situation, right? I broke her once. I don’t have the right to touch even her shadow now.”

“I just keep staring at her like a fool… but the problem is—”

“No one knows when your Beauty Queen turns back into Jhansi ki Rani again.”

“So I sit here. Quietly. Just thanking God she’s here. Happy. Glowing. Alive.”

Yatharva simply smiled with halwa on his cheeks.

And in that moment — despite the laughter, the teasing, the food, the noise — **Vihan’s world had shrunk to one woman… and the child who might one day call him Dad.**

Chapter 16: The Gift That Broke the Silence

The dinner plates were almost empty, the bowls being passed around slower now, as people shifted from eating to talking. The laughter still echoed, and the gajar ka halwa was down to its final spoonfuls.

In the middle of all this, **Anjali quietly looked up at Vihan** — still feeding bits to Yatharva, still sitting a little reserved, still *watching but never asking.*

She took a breath, sipped her water, and said in her calm, warm voice:

"You're doing good, man."

Vihan looked at her — surprised.

She smiled, gently.
"Actually… you're doing the *best* you've ever done."

The room fell a little quiet.

Everyone subtly turned their attention toward her.

"And… thank you so much."
She looked down at her plate, then back at him.
"Also yes, I'm sorry… for being so rude that day. It's just…"

She paused.

"You know what I mean."

Vihan nodded slowly. His throat tightened.

"But really, thank you," she said again, voice a little softer this time.

"And yes… I got something for you."

Vihan blinked.

"For me?"

She smirked, wiping her hands on a tissue.

"Yup. I'll show you after dinner."

After Dinner — The Sound That Stole Everyone's Breath

As everyone got up, stretching and walking toward the drawing room, Anjali pulled out her phone.

With a knowing smile, she **dialed a number.**

Suddenly…
"DHADAAAMMMMMM…!!"

The sound of a **roaring Bullet bike** echoed from outside the main gate.

Everyone — startled, confused, excited — rushed to the front door.

The sisters screamed. The house help ran with their phones ready.

And then they saw it.

A brand-new Royal Enfield Bullet, shining in black and chrome, rolled up by a delivery guy.

The plate read:
"Vihan Pandit – Ride with Purpose"

His favorite bike. His dream.
Standing right in front of him.

He stood **speechless**.

The world blurred.

Anjali walked up beside him, arms folded.

"Hey..." she said casually.
"How's it? You like it or not? It's okay if you don't… I'll return it. We'll get you something else."

She said it lightly.
But her voice… was full of nerves. Emotion. Fear. Love.

Vihan's eyes welled up instantly.
He took a step back. Covered his mouth.

And then without warning —
he pulled her into the tightest hug.

In front of everyone.

"I love you," he whispered.
"This… is the best gift of my life."

"You still remembered," he said, choking on his tears,
"what would make me feel alive."

The family stood frozen for a moment.

And then — everyone clapped.

Someone yelled **"Areeee proposal ho gaya kyaaaa!!"**
(*"Wait... is this a proposal happening?!"*)

Phones flashed. Videos were made.

On His Knees — One More Time

Vihan stepped back slowly.

His eyes locked on hers.

He bent down on one knee — **again** — in the same place where her pain once began.

He opened his palm, holding nothing but his truth.

**"I know I lost all my chances… but I'll still try.
I'm sorry. For everything.
If not your love… give me a place where I can protect you, laugh with you, and heal what I broke."**

Anjali stood still.

Eyes slightly glossy.
Hands shaking.
Lips trembling.

She looked at the crowd, then at him — on one knee.

And for a second… **she almost gave in**.

Almost.

But then… **she stepped back.**

Ignored her own trembling heart.

Turned silently.

And walked away.

The Aftermath

The house grew quiet.

Everyone watched her go — confused, emotional, some with tears, some in silence.

Vihan stayed kneeling for a moment longer.

Then stood up, wiping his tears.

Anjali's mother walked up, placed her hand on his shoulder.

**"Beta… she's not rejecting you.
She's just… scared of breaking again."**

**"Give her time.
This is the most beautiful chaos we've had in this house in years."**

Her father, uncle, and sister had already gone behind Anjali, trying to talk to her, listen, hold space.

Vihan?
He didn't chase her.

He just stood there.

And smiled through the ache.

The house help brought him water.
One gently wiped his kurta sleeve.
Another patted his back.

In that moment, **he wasn't just a man in love.**

He was family.

Bruised. Waiting.
But **finally… accepted.**

Chapter 17 -The Dilema, the self realization and apologies

That night, after all the chaos, claps, and the heartbreak of her silent departure, **Vihan sat in the corner of the verandah**, staring at the moonlight slipping through the neem tree.

He had stopped wiping his tears. He'd stopped checking his phone too.

After a long, quiet conversation with **Anjali's mother**, where she reassured him that love doesn't disappear, it just *freezes when it's hurt*, Vihan nodded, stood up, and walked out into the cool air.

And then he did the only thing he could think of —
He called Ronie.

Vihan & Ronie — The Phone Call

Ronie picked up on the second ring.

"Bhai..." Vihan whispered, his voice rough.

"Kya haal hai?" (How are you?)

"There's no hope left, Ronie."
"I've ruined it beyond anything I could ever repair."

Ronie sighed.

"Bhai, don't say that—"

"No, listen. I thought maybe... just maybe, she'd say yes. That moment, when I was on my knees... it felt real. Her eyes softened. But then she left."

"And I get it. Because the moment I say the word *love*, she travels back. Back to the insults, the shouting, the abandonment. To all the pain that *I* gave her."

"So from today… I'll stop being her lover. I'll stop expecting." "I'll just try to be… her friend."

He hung up before Ronie could say anything else.

Then opened his phone.

And typed.
Typed again.
Deleted.
Typed again.

And then, in one sitting — **he sent her messages. Dozens of them. Long ones. Raw ones. Soft ones.**

Apologies not just for the night before, but for years.

For the station insults. For the ignored tears. For the unanswered texts. For the hospital visits she made alone.

For the version of him that once existed.

And the only promise he made now?

"Main sirf dost banna chahta hoon. No expectations. No pressure. Just… let me be someone who protects you without making you feel trapped."
(*"I only want to be your friend now…"*)

Meanwhile: A New Morning, The Same Queen

The next morning, **Anjali's room smelled of sandalwood and tulsi leaves**.

She had woken up early — like always.
But unlike the emotional whirlwind of the night before, her face was calm. Almost peaceful.

Anjali's Morning: Stronger Than Storms

The sun peeked through the sheer curtains, casting gold ribbons on the marble floor.

Anjali woke up in quiet. No alarm. Just the soft stir of the house waking with her.

She reached for her cup of tea on the side table. It was warm — her mother had already sent it in.

She sat by the window, sipping slowly, **her mind strangely still**.

No replay of last night. No running thoughts. Just… calm.

After finishing her tea, she took her towel and walked to bathe — letting the cool water ground her, washing away not just the sweat and stress, but **the clutter in her chest.**

She changed into a soft **pale cotton saree**, tied her damp hair into a neat bun, wore a **small black bindi**, and fastened her **silver wristwatch** — the one she had gifted herself after clearing UPSC.

Her steps were light, her expression peaceful.

She walked into the inner prayer room of the mansion — a quiet, sacred corner filled with marigold garlands and sandalwood scent.

There, she sat cross-legged, eyes closed, palms joined.

She began her **Durga Saptashati Paath**, her voice steady, sacred.

Each verse like a whisper to her inner strength.
Each chant a salve to wounds that still throbbed.

Then the **Shiva Stotra** followed — a surrender. A reminder that even the most powerful must sometimes just… breathe.

She wasn't healing because things were better.

She was healing because **she had chosen peace over chaos, silence over conflict.**

Yatharva – Her Sunshine

After prayer, she walked into the living room where **Yatharva** was already crawling around in his soft **malmal kurta and half-pants**, squealing happily as her father tried to teach him to clap to a bhajan.

"**Maa-ma! Maa-maaa!**" he kept trying, stumbling on little feet, throwing his tiny arms at everything that moved.

Whenever someone tickled him, his giggles rang like temple bells — **pure, divine, freeing.**

Anjali's mother walked in with mashed banana in a bowl.
Her sisters video-called from abroad, taking turns to ask, *"Kya word bola aaj?"* ("What new word did he say today?")

"Omg look at his kurta! Did you sew that, Di?"

Yes.
She did.

In her free time — sometimes past midnight — Anjali would **design and sew his clothes herself**, choosing soft pastel fabrics, gentle threads, and stitching them with the same care she used to stitch her broken soul.

He looked **happy. Healthy. Whole.**
He looked like **everything she wanted him to become** — a boy who'd grow up with music, shlokas, long drives, and a heart full of both strength and softness.

Anjali smiled.

She hadn't smiled like this in weeks.

Her **Tau ji** played soft tabla beats.
Her father taught him to bow to the idol after eating.

Yatharva was becoming everything she had dreamed of — not just happy, but whole. With values, laughter, and love all around him.

In the chaos of baby giggles, toy rattles, bhajan beats, and motherly eyes — **Anjali's smile found its way back.**

Vihan's Messages – Waiting Unread

As she finally took a break, wiping baby food off her saree, she picked up her phone — nearly 30 unread texts blinking at her.

She sighed.
Scrolled.

All from Vihan.

Each one… heavy.
Some full of shame.
Some full of care.
None demanding anything.

Only the last one remained unread for a few seconds longer.

She clicked it.

"I know you won't reply. And that's okay.
I just want you to know —
This version of me…
Isn't here to get you back.
Just to make sure you never fall again, even if I'm not the one holding you."

She didn't reply.

But she didn't delete the messages either.

She just sat there, hugging Yatharva a little tighter — her baby cooing in her arms, his tiny hands tapping her cheeks.

And through that tiny touch, **she let herself feel loved… even if she wasn't ready to return it yet.**

Chapter 18: When the Strongest Fell

After almost a month,It happened without warning.

Anjali collapsed in the middle of the hall.
No sound. No scream. Just her tea cup falling from her hand… and her body going limp onto the floor.

The house froze.

"Anjali!!!" her mother shouted, running toward her.

The staff, her sisters, her father — everyone rushed in.

Vihan was the first to reach. He held her head in his lap, his hands trembling.

"Breathe… Anjali… please…"

Her eyes were shut.

Her face pale.

She wasn't moving.

The Hospital Panic

They rushed her to the **biggest hospital in the district**.

Emergency lights. Oxygen tubes. Doctors pushing stretchers. Machines beeping.

Everyone outside was in silence.

Anjali's mother stood still. Guilt written all over her face.

"I shouldn't have encouraged Vihan… I thought she was strong enough… but maybe I added pressure," she whispered to herself, breaking down.

Others began to feel the same. No one said it aloud, but their eyes pointed toward **Vihan** — now sitting in the corridor, his hands clenched, his tears falling freely.

He had **lost control of his voice**.
He kept asking the same thing to every nurse, every doctor:

"Will she be okay? Please tell me she'll be okay. When will she open her eyes again?"

And every answer came with just one helpless line:

"Only God knows. She's not just a patient… she's the soul of this city."

Diagnosis: The Weight of Too Much

Later that night, the doctor came out, removing his gloves, his face heavy.

"Long-term emotional and mental trauma," he said.
"She's been carrying too much. For too long."

"The mind has a limit. And hers… crossed it."

"We need to keep her here for a long time. Maybe years. Because her nervous system isn't responding normally to treatment anymore."

Everyone gasped.

No one spoke.

And Vihan… **shattered silently.**

The Waiting Room Routine

It became a **new normal**.

Family members would visit every day — some in the morning, some in the evening.

Yatharva, now almost a year old, would come once a week, brought by her mother, just to sit next to her. He didn't understand why she wasn't hugging him back.

Vihan never missed a day.
Never left the district.

He started sleeping on the bench near her room. **His beard had grown. Hair too.**

Her mother once handed him a razor and said softly,
"Beta, shave kar lo. You're scaring the kids."

He smiled weakly. **"Main theek tab lagunga jab Anjali theek hogi."**
(*"I'll look fine the day she becomes fine."*)

And he never did shave.

In the background, he also continued **calling, threatening, and confronting** every person who had ever insulted, harassed, or broken Anjali — relentlessly.

"You destroyed her with your words. She's in a hospital because of you. Start writing your apologies, or I swear, I'll make you feel every ounce of guilt you threw at her."

He made sure they understood what they had done.

Days passed, but the guilt inside **Vihan** never did.

He had accepted that love may never return… but he wasn't done yet. Not until **every person** who broke Anjali — including himself — was held accountable.

And then… it happened.

A call. A snide remark.
A woman from his past — one of those who had once slapped Anjali, blamed her, mocked her character — called again.

Laughing. Pretending.

Saying things like,

"Beta, tum toh usi ladki ke liye pagal ho gaye? Arre, woh toh waise bhi characterless thi… yaad hai na?"
(*"Son, you've gone crazy for that girl? She was always characterless… don't you remember?"*)

And something inside Vihan **snapped.**

The Call That Turned Into Fire

He dialed every single one of them. The family members. The neighbors. The woman. The relatives.

Screamed. Cried. Roared.

"YOU made her life a nightmare!"

"You judged her, raised hands on her, questioned her dignity — and *I* stood there like a coward."

"She is hard now. Cold. Unreachable. Why? Because you turned her soft heart into stone!"

"She still cries thinking about how people once called her names, doubted her intentions, judged her character when all she did was love and sacrifice."

Then he shouted into the phone, voice shaking:

"She COULD have taken revenge. She COULD have crushed all of us with her power — she's an IAS officer now! But no."

"She chose to heal. To work on herself. And still smiled like nothing happened."

His voice broke.

"And you… you call her characterless?"

"You're not humans. You're demons. And I was the biggest demon of all."

The old woman on the line — the one who once raised her hand on Anjali — tried her old tricks.

“Beta… you know I never meant it that way. She was always too proud. Too opinionated—”

“SHUT UP!” Vihan roared.

“Don’t 'beta' me. Don’t ever try to sugarcoat what you did. I may have respected you once. But not anymore.”

“You’re older, yes. But that doesn’t give you the right to destroy someone’s mental peace.”

And then… the final blow.

“You better prepare your apology. All of you.
Because when Anjali opens her eyes again…
You’ll come. One by one. And bow your head.
Or I swear — I’ll burn every fake relationship to ashes.”

He hung up.

And exhaled.

The Look in His Eyes

And when the dust settled…

She saw him.

Vihan.

Always nearby.
Never in her way.
Eyes full of guilt.
And **overflowing with silent love**.

He didn’t touch her hand.
He didn’t say "I love you" again.

He just looked at her like **he finally understood who she was.**

And that was the first time…
Anjali looked back.

And smiled.

Not because she had to.

But because **she was proud of him.**

One Year Later… A Ray of Light

It had been **close to a year**.

Anjali hadn't walked the corridors of her mansion. She hadn't spoken in her powerful voice. She hadn't heard her son call her name.

But today… something was different.

Discharge papers were being signed.

Anjali had begun responding.

She wasn't fully recovered. Her body was still fragile. Her eyes still had shadows. But she could walk. She could eat. She could whisper.

She was ready to go home.

Yatharva was 1.5 years old now. Running, talking in half-sentences, calling names. His eyes sparkled when he saw her.

And when he ran into her arms in the hospital room, the entire family broke down.

She held him close. Buried her face in his hair. And didn't let go.

Vihan stood quietly in the corner, watching.

His beard now thick, his shirt slightly loose, his hands trembling.

He had written **365 diary entries** — one for each day she had been unconscious.

He never showed them to anyone.

But today… he slipped the last one into her hospital bag.

Page 365: "You're back. I'll start breathing now."

After months in recovery, when Anjali finally came home fully conscious, walking with strength again — something had changed in her eyes.

She was calm. Peaceful.
But also… lighter.

And what surprised her even more?

She received video messages. Texts. Apologies.
From people she never expected to hear from.

People who once humiliated her.
Now sending voice notes and messages with folded hands.
Saying sorry. Admitting guilt.

One by one, they came to her mansion.

Some couldn't meet her eyes.
Some cried.
Some just touched her feet.

And Anjali?

She stood silent for a few seconds each time…
Then folded her hands and softly said:
"Theek hai. Aap maafi maang chuke. Bas yaad rakhiye — kisi ki izzat aapke shabdon se na tooti jaye."
(*"Alright. You've apologized. Just remember — don't let your words break someone else's dignity again."*)

She didn't hug them.
Didn't offer tea.

But she forgave.

Not for them — **for herself.**

The Healing After the Storm

Anjali had been unwell — her health had collapsed under emotional pressure. **It took nearly a year** for her to fully recover.

She missed Yatharva's first birthday.

But **Vihan didn't let the house feel empty.**
He organized a beautiful, warm celebration with the family, clicked pictures, and lit candles with Yatharva's little hands.

And throughout those months…
He never left.

He helped the staff. Took care of medicines.
Sat outside her room, sometimes the whole night.
Didn't ask for attention.
Didn't beg for love.

He just… **showed up.** Every single day.

And the family saw it.

Anjali's father watched quietly. Her mother silently forgave him. Her sisters — especially the ones abroad — started warming up.

And one day, after dinner, her uncle smiled and said:

"Let's just get them married. The boy is already a son. Why not make it official before the other daughters get married?"

Everyone smiled.

Even her mother.

Chapter 19: Forgiveness Wrapped in Tea and Laughter

It had been two months since **Anjali came back home from the hospital**.

The storm was over — outside, at least.

But healing? Healing was still **quiet**, happening in stolen silences, soft smiles, and small efforts from everyone.

She no longer needed help walking. She had started taking her own tea again. Her sarees were no longer pale hospital tones, but calm, earthy colors. The pooja corner had her soft humming again. **Life was returning — one morning at a time.**

And **Vihan**?

Still the same.

Still writing in his **diary every night**, pages filled with unsaid thoughts, sketches of Yatharva, pressed flowers, and little notes he wished he could say aloud.

He never gave her the diary.

But **she found it anyway.**

And one evening, when the house was asleep and the wind was soft, she sat by the window and read every single page.

From the guilt.
To the pain.
To the days he cursed himself for breaking her.
To the mornings he begged the universe to keep her alive.
To the nights he sat by her hospital bed, just watching her breathe.

By the time she closed the diary, **her eyes were wet.**

But her heart?

Lighter.
Ready.

The Morning of the Hug

It was just like any other morning. Vihan, as usual, knocked lightly on her room door and entered with a cup of tea in his hand.

But before he could place it on the table, **Anjali looked up and softly said:**

"Vihan… baitho zara."
(*"Vihan... sit for a minute."*)

He looked up, a little surprised, but sat.

And without a word, she reached out… and **hugged him. Tight. Silent. Warm. Long.**

He froze for a moment.

Then slowly, **closed his eyes and melted into the embrace** — like the version of himself he had been waiting to be… had finally been born.

At the door, **her mother stood silently**, watching the scene with misty eyes.

She smiled softly and whispered to herself:
"I think… she's forgiven him. She's okay now."

Then turned and went downstairs with the biggest smile in months.

The Diary Confession

Anjali gently pulled away from the hug but still held his hand.

"Sorry…" she said.
"But I read your diary."

Vihan's eyes widened.

"What?! You—"
His voice stopped. Then softened.

"I mean… it was private, but… I'm glad you did."

She smiled and whispered:

"I didn't want to forgive you with words… I wanted to understand your pain first. Now I do."

He looked down, voice trembling.

"I was scared every day. Scared that I lost you again… and this time because of me."

She shook her head gently.
"No, pagal…" she smiled.
"It was life. And your efforts didn't go waste. I got the apology messages too. It's over now. And I'm… ready to close that chapter."

Vihan blinked.

Smiled.

And **hugged her back**, not like a lover — but like a man who was finally at peace.

The Teasing That Followed

Just then, **his phone rang.**

On speaker.

It was Anjali's mother.

"Ahem… ab meri beti ko chhed liya ho toh neeche aa jao! Uski maa bhi ghar mein hai, aur baaki sab bude buzurg bhi hain. Dono neeche aa jao!"
(*"If you're done flirting with my daughter, come downstairs now! Her mother is still alive — and the elders are too! Both of you, downstairs!"*)

The phone's volume was high.

Anjali heard everything.

She turned red instantly. Vihan looked at her with a grin, equally embarrassed.

"Main dekhta hoon…" he muttered and rushed downstairs like a schoolboy caught sneaking out.

Downstairs – The Breakfast of Happiness

The fragrance of **ajwain parathas, fresh halwa, and adrak wali chai** filled the air.

The breakfast table was buzzing.

Sisters laughing, uncles reading newspapers, staff serving with smiles.

Yatharva sat on his "bade naanu's" lap, stuffing halwa into his cheeks, giggling.

And then…

Anjali entered.

In a crisp blue saree, hair neatly tied, bindi perfectly placed — **not a patient anymore. A queen, once again.**

Everyone clapped softly, like welcoming the sun after a long night.

She smiled, took her seat beside her sisters, and poured herself tea.

And Then… The Teasing Took Over

As the parathas were being passed around, her sisters began teasing:

"Didi… toh ab honeymoon trip ka plan bhi banana hai kya?"
"Kaunsa day fix karein engagement ka?"
"Waise Vihan ke daant clean karwa do, shaadi ke pics ache aayenge!"

Anjali rolled her eyes.

"Bas karo!" she laughed.
"Waise tum log apne hone wale patiyon ko bulao… shaadi ki dates fix karni hain."

Before her sisters could reply…

Yatharva, mouth full of halwa, shouted in his kiddish voice:

"Haan! Lao! Jaldi lao! Mumma mujhe naye kapde milenge na?"

The entire table **burst into laughter.**

Anjali smiled wide, shaking her head.

Her sisters grinned and said,
"Okay Di! Meeting tomorrow. Final!"

Chapter 20: The Interview Before the I Do

The mansion had turned into a **festival of colors and excitement**.

Now that Anjali had recovered and returned to her routine — with peace in her heart and forgiveness behind her — it was time to **move forward with the rest of the family's dreams.**

And right at the top of that list?
Her sisters' weddings.

After a few weeks of playful warnings, **her sisters had finally brought their would-be husbands home** — for a proper introduction.

Not just for the family…

But for "DM Madam" herself.

The drawing room was set.

Four nervous boys sat side by side on the couch, sweating not because of the heat — but because of **Anjali's presence**.

In her crisp saree, hair tied neatly, and diary in hand — she wasn't behaving like their soon-to-be sister-in-law…

She looked like a panel judge. IAS interview style.

The Dads Make It Official

Her **father and Tau ji** entered with a smile and sat on the other side.

Her father said with a smirk,
"Dekho bhai, jo bhi ho, hamari betiyon ki shaadi ki baat toh… hamara beta hi karega."
(*"Look, whatever happens, the final talk about our daughters' marriages will be done by our son."*)

And he turned to look at…

Anjali.

All eyes followed.

The boys looked even more scared.

She lifted her eyes from the diary and said calmly,
"Toh shuru karein?"
(*"Shall we begin?"*)

They nodded like schoolboys.

The IAS-Style Interview

Anjali went one by one:

"Aap kis field mein hain?" (*"What's your profession?"*)

"Future planning ka kya vision hai?" (*"What's your vision for the future?"*)

"Ghar ke mamle kaise sambhalte ho?" (*"How do you handle family matters?"*)

"Apni fiancé ko kab aakhri baar compliment diya tha?" (*"When was the last time you complimented your fiancée?"*)

Their faces turned pink.

Everyone else watched like it was a live court hearing. Even the family cook paused by the door.

Anjali closed her diary.

"Bas ek kaam karo… jaake sab ke liye chai bana lao."
(*"Just do one thing... go make tea for everyone."*)

The boys stood up **immediately** and nodded in sync. **"Yes ma'am!"**

As they turned to walk toward the kitchen — worried, quiet, almost trembling — she spoke again.

"Ruko. Baith jao."
(*"Stop. Sit down."*)

They froze mid-step.

Sisters Panic, Vihan Enters the Chat

In the corner of the room, **Anjali's sisters panicked**.

One sister quickly typed a message to Vihan:

"Jijuuuu! What is happening?! Why is Di being soooo strict? Please do something!"

Another one added:

"Bro she's interviewing them like they're joining RAW or NASA! Save them before they faint!"

Vihan, standing near the kitchen with a cup of tea, chuckled and **forwarded the message to Anjali.**

"Ma'am, urgent message. Please have a look."

She looked at the phone screen.

Saw the messages.

And… stood up.

The Final Verdict

She looked at the four boys — still seated, trying not to breathe too loudly.

She took a long pause, pacing like a judge in a courtroom.

Then she said clearly:

"Suno tum chaaron…"
(*"Listen, you four…"*)

"Tumhare pasand kiye gaye ladke…"
(*"The boys you all have chosen…"*)

Everyone leaned in.

The sisters stared with wide eyes. The boys almost held their breath.

She paused again.

And then—

She **burst into laughter**, her eyes sparkling.

"Hume pasand hain!"
(*"I approve of them!"*)

Everyone gasped — then exploded into claps and cheers.

"Pandit ji ko bulao! Sabki families ko phone lagao! Let's fix the marriage dates AS SOON AS POSSIBLE!"

Laughter. Joy. Relief.

The boys finally exhaled. The sisters jumped off the sofas to hug her. Anjali's mother joined in with tears and kisses. Vihan smiled from the corner, watching the love of his life, *being the soul of her home.*

Chapter 21: Shaadi Ki Shuruaat (Beginning of the wedding mood)— Mangoes, Mandates, and Masti!

After the teasing, interviews, and laughter-filled approvals, the house buzzed with a new energy — **wedding preparation mode was ON.**

Anjali's father picked up his phone and called **his Guruji** with folded hands and deep respect.

"Guruji, ab sab kuch theek hai. Hum chahte hain ki shaadiyon ki tareekh aap hi nirdharit karein."
(*"Guruji, now that everything is in place, we would like you to finalize the wedding dates yourself."*)

Standing nearby, **Anjali smiled and said softly:**

"Papa, I think it would be better if *you* go and bring him home yourself. He'll feel respected."

Her father looked at her proudly and nodded.
"Theek hai bitiya, main chalta hoon." (*"Alright, daughter, I'll go."*)

He left with the driver, while **Anjali went back to coordinating everything like the silent captain she was.**

Next Morning: Dates Locked & Rituals Begin

The next morning, **Guruji arrived**, greeted with tilak and flowers.

Along with him, **the would-be grooms' families also came** — smiling, hopeful, warmly dressed in simple yet elegant clothes.

Everyone gathered in the main hall. Chai, nimbu paani, snacks, laughter — the entire house shimmered with positive energy.

Tika and engagement dates were fixed.

The mothers gave **sarees and dupattas** to their soon-to-be daughters-in-law — a symbolic blessing for the new journey.

Photographs were taken. Blessings were exchanged.

And after everything — a beautiful home-cooked **meal was served to everyone**. Laughter filled every corner. People were seated in pairs, chatting about lehengas, venues, and barat dances.

The Family Moments

Yatharva wandered from lap to lap — sometimes with a sweet in his hand, sometimes holding a spoon he stole from the kitchen.

Tau ji and Papa sat proudly in the corner, sipping chai, their eyes soaking in the happiness.

"Dekha? Hamari Anjali ne sab sambhal liya," said Tau ji.
(*"See? Our Anjali managed everything perfectly."*)

Anjali's mother, emotional but glowing with peace, nodded silently — watching the daughter she once cried for, now surrounded by love, health, and joy.

Meanwhile, **Anjali and Vihan** were in a corner, sorting out final gift packs, coordinating return favors, and listing next-day tasks.

Suddenly—

"Beta, tum dono aa jao ab. Baitho sabke saath."
(*"Kids, you both come now. Sit with everyone."*)
Tau ji called out.

Anjali, while sealing a gift box, replied:

"Ok, ok… bas do minute. Aati hoon."
(*"Just give me 2 mins. I'm coming."*)

Then she looked at Vihan and nodded.

"Tum jao. I'll join you in a bit."

Mango Shake and June Heat

She walked to the kitchen entrance and called out:

"Kaka! Badiya sa mango shake ho jaayega kya sabke liye? Garmi kaafi ho gayi hai."
(*"Kaka, can we get some good mango shake for everyone? It's too hot today."*)

From inside the kitchen came a loud laugh and response:

"Arre bitiya! Kaisi baat kar di! Das minute mein aata hai sabke liye — ekdum thanda thanda!"
(*"What are you saying, child! It'll be ready in 10 minutes — chilled and perfect!"*)

Anjali smiled. It felt like home again.

The Group Plan Begins

Back in the living area, everyone was laughing and joking when **Vihan stood up and said:**

"I think now we should start planning wedding shopping too. August is right around the corner — we don't have much time."

Everyone agreed instantly.

Anjali's sisters looked at each other, smirked, and said loudly:

"I think our perfect wedding planner is sitting right here — *Mr. Vihan*, didi ka dost!"
(*"Sister's friend Mr. Vihan would be perfect to lead us!"*)

Everyone laughed. Vihan mock bowed and said:

"Challenge accepted. But on one condition — we finalize the shopping spots now, and plan everything around weekends."

He took out his phone, grinned, and said:

"Also, I'm making a WhatsApp group… name will be: 'Shaadi Ki Shopping Aur Masti!'"

There was a round of cheers and claps.

Numbers were exchanged. Cousins were added. A group call was made, and Vihan, like a true planner, invited everyone:

"Be ready this weekend! Shopping, masti, and chaos — here we come!"

The whole house echoed with laughter.

And Anjali… Finally Exhaled

Standing at the kitchen entrance, watching everyone smile, laugh, and joke — **Anjali finally took a deep breath.**

No anxiety. No weight. No hesitation.

Just… **peace.**

Her **father, Tau ji, and mother** stood behind her, watching with the same pride they felt the day she cracked her UPSC.

"Dekha?" her mother whispered. "Woh phir se muskurane lagi hai."
(*"See? She's smiling again."*)

And this time… the smile was for real.

Chapter 22: Weekend Planning, Wedding Vibes, and the Return of Laughter

Saturday morning arrived with extra sunshine, louder laughter, and the kind of energy only a shaadi-waala weekend brings.

The courtyard of Anjali's house was already alive by 9 AM — cousins from nearby cities had arrived, suitcases dumped in the hall, and everyone had one thing on their mind:

"Let's make this shaadi memorable from Day 1!"

In the middle of the buzz, **Vihan stood with a notepad and chai**, waiting for all the cousins to settle.

As soon as everyone gathered, he stood up and announced:

"Okay team — priority one: Documentation!"

Everyone blinked.

He smiled.

"We need a wedding photographer and videographer who'll record everything — from the planning, the shopping, the madness — not just the final day. A story from the very beginning."

The cousins cheered.

"Yesss! Wedding vlog types! Let's goooo!"

Planning, Step by Step

After that, **Vihan ticked off the next points:**

→□ Photographer — check
→□ Card printer — next
→□ Then visit and finalize wedding venues

But before anything else, he said:

"We need to call in the big bosses — all mommies, papas, tau jis, and the lovely ladies with veto power."

He winked. Everyone laughed.

The Elders' Inputs

Soon, the elders joined in the living room, sitting with tea, murmuring among themselves.

Vihan stood at the front and said:

"Venue preferences, please?"

Anjali's mother spoke first:
"Beta, bas ethnic ho… aur thoda spacious. Baaki hum flexible hain."

One aunt added:
"Haan, stage acha hona chahiye. Dance ka jagah ho."

Her father smiled:
"Baaki sab tum log sambhalo, bas shaadi shaan se honi chahiye."

Vihan noted everything, looked around and said:

"All done! Leave it to us now."

Everyone clapped and moved on to gossip and chai.

Cousins' Plan: Delegation Mode ON

After the meeting, all the cousins gathered again.

One cousin whispered:

"Bro… Anjali di is the best when it comes to managing events."
"Honestly, we're not cut out for all the venue-decoration-menu drama."
"Vihan bhaiya, you and Anjali di handle that part, please!"

Another cousin said dramatically:

"Hume toh bas photos, shaadi cards, khaana aur kapde chahiye."

All nodded in agreement.

Vihan laughed and mock-saluted them.

"Done. Tum log masti karo, photos lo, khaana khao. Management is on us."

The Weekend That Felt Like a Movie

Saturday and Sunday were packed.

□ **The photography team was booked** — they even did a mini shoot of the entire family at the house, capturing those silly, chaotic behind-the-scenes moments.

💌 **The card printer was finalised**, and everyone selected one elegant ethnic design with gold foil — simple, timeless.

👗 **The cousins, after that, disappeared** into boutiques, cafes, and malls — trying on sherwanis, lehengas, taking mirror selfies, laughing over overpriced chaat.

□□ They ended every evening with food — roadside momos, kulfi at 11 PM, late-night chai under fairy lights.

Meanwhile…

Anjali and Vihan, like the calm captains of this storm, managed every logistics, booked appointments, finalised caterers, and even did budget breakdowns — all without losing their minds.

Their synergy was smooth.
No arguments.
No clashes.
Just silent support and shared smiles.

Sometimes, all it takes is a quiet glance between two people to know:

"We've been through worse. This joy? We've earned it."

Chapter 23: Yatharva Turns Two, Vedic Vows Begin

The mansion woke up that day with a softness in the air — a calm, sacred kind of joy. It wasn't the chaos of a wedding, nor the noise of an official event.
It was the **birthday of the heartbeat of the house**.

Yatharva had turned two.

Two years of light.
Two years of laughter, strength, and survival.
And today, the house was glowing — not just in lights, but in love.

A Celebration of Life, Not Just a Birthday

Anjali had kept it intimate, simple, and close to tradition.

No cartoon theme. No loud DJ.

Instead, the garden was decorated with **marigolds, mango leaves, mud pots, rangoli, and hand-painted wooden toys**. There were fairy lights wrapped around banana stems, and handmade return gifts wrapped in cotton fabric.

Yatharva wore a white malmal kurta-pajama with light orange embroidery, designed by Anjali herself and stitched by the local tailor she trusted the most.

As she held him close while he cut the millet-jaggery cake, surrounded by claps and soft shehnai music, she whispered:

"Happy birthday, mera chhota suraj..."
(*"Happy birthday, my little sun..."*)

He clapped along with everyone, his tiny palms smudged with cake, his eyes twinkling like a thousand diyas.

It wasn't just his birthday.

It was a reminder to everyone present — **of life after pain. Of light after storms.**

And Then Came the Weddings…

With his birthday celebrated with grace and warmth, the house flowed right into the **next wave of joy — wedding time.**

All three of Anjali's sisters were now preparing for their new chapters.

And at the center of it all — with a diary in hand and peace in her smile — stood **Anjali.**

Anjali's Touch — From Fabric to Feelings

Every element of the wedding carried **her heart and her healing**.

She personally designed all the **wedding outfits**, down to the thread.

Men were to wear **dhoti-kurtas**, with natural color blocks and Vedic motifs.
Women and girls were styled in **temple-border sarees** in earthy pastels — **handwoven, light, and stunning.**

And once again, the same **local tailor** who had sewn Yatharva's birthday outfit was now the creator of the groom's attire.

"The wedding should empower more than just the couple," Anjali had told her sisters.

The Venue — Simplicity Meets Soul

The venue was a spiritual canvas.

Everything was natural — **brass, banana leaves, clay pots, tulsi plants, handmade diyas, turmeric drapes.**

There was **no plastic anywhere**.

Chants of **Rigvedic hymns**, soft instrumental music, and the fragrance of sandalwood created an atmosphere that wasn't just aesthetic — it was **divine**.

Guests walked in and felt something sacred — something missing from most weddings.

And the **menu?**

It was sattvik, organic, and rooted in heritage — millet laddoos, ghee-cooked sabzis, kachoris, chaach, tulsi drinks, all served on leaf plates and copper glasses.

Nothing wasted.

Leftover food was **donated to orphanages, old-age homes, and gaushalas**, as Anjali had arranged with the local food support team in advance.

A Wedding That Made Headlines

What started as a family affair soon caught national attention.

By next morning, their wedding was featured in **magazines, social media pages, and state news channels**.

"A Vedic Wedding Without Plastic — IAS Anjali's Family Sets a Powerful Example"
"Dignity in Simplicity: The District Wedding Everyone's Talking About"

But in the house, none of that mattered.

Because peace had returned.

The elders were smiling.
The newlyweds were glowing.
And Anjali — finally — was breathing with ease.

Back to Calm — And a Friday to Look Forward To

After the **vidai**, things returned to their gentle pace.

Evenings with chai.
Soft laughter in the hallway.
Yatharva running around with a new toy every day.

And now, the next excitement?
Pag-phere.

All three sisters were set to return to **Anjali's mansion** that coming **Friday**, and the house was already planning for their arrival.

Sweets, thaalis, little surprises — and Anjali, as always, was preparing quietly — smiling to herself as she wrote their names on return gifts with haldi and sindoor designs.

Because this time, they weren't just coming back as sisters.

They were coming back as women ready for their own stories.

Chapter 24: Pag-Phera, Love & Lovely Satires

(Pyaar & Pyar Bhare Taane)

Friday morning came with the aroma of desi ghee in the air.

Anjali had personally instructed the kitchen staff to prepare **dal baati, churma, kheer, and aloo-puri** — all the favorites of her sisters. The thaalis were decorated with kumkum, turmeric, and mogra petals.

The **entrance of the mansion was decorated in soft yellow and maroon**. A rangoli made by the house helps bloomed like a lotus, and brass diyas flickered at the threshold.

At 11 AM sharp — **they arrived.**

All three sisters — now brides — walked into the home laughing, holding their lehengas, and shouting:

"Didi! We're back... and married now! Ready to boss around!"

Behind them, their husbands followed like nervous newcomers on the first day of school.

Anjali smiled softly and came to the door, holding a kalash and pooja thali.
She touched their heads gently one by one and whispered:

"Swagat hai, nayi dulhano. Par yaad rahe, tum ab bhi meri chhoti behne ho."
(*"Welcome, new brides. But remember, you're still my little sisters."*)

Everyone laughed.

Teasing, Tandoor & Thalis

The dining table was full — food steaming, glasses clinking, laughter rising and falling like music.

Tau ji and Papa sat proudly at the head of the table.
Anjali's mom kept placing extra sweets into everyone's bowls despite protest.
Yatharva ran from lap to lap like a prince inspecting his court.

And Vihan?

Helping serve water. Making sure every plate had everything. Quiet, involved, glowing.

The Sisters Strike Again

After lunch, while the men sat down for chai, **the sisters gathered in Anjali's room**, sitting cross-legged on her bed, just like old times.

One of them nudged her and said:

"Didi... let's stop the suspense. Tell us. What's your story now?"

Another chimed in:

"Look around. Weddings done. You're smiling again. Vihan bhaiya looks like he'll pass any 'ghar ka damaad' interview. Toh ab kya soch rahi ho?"

Anjali smiled, looking down at her hands.

"Soch toh rahi hoon..." she said softly.
(*"I am thinking..."*)

"Bas... is baar decisions sirf dil se hongi. Samajh se nahi."
(*"This time, my decisions will be made from the heart, not logic."*)

There was silence. Not because they were shocked — but because they understood.

Finally, **the eldest sister, the warrior, the DM... was letting her guard down.**

A Quiet Conversation Outside

Later that evening, after the rituals, photos, and cousin reels were done, Anjali stepped out into the verandah for some fresh air. The sky was soft pink, and the lights had started twinkling again.

Vihan joined her silently, holding two steel glasses of chai.

He offered her one.

She took it, smiled, and asked:

"Tired?"

"Not at all," he replied, eyes kind.
"This feels like home now."

She looked up at him.

"It is your home. And… thank you."

He blinked. **"For what?"**

"For not walking away this time."

He didn't reply. Just smiled, and they sipped chai in silence.

Chapter 25: The Last Yes — When Love Asks, "Are You Ready?"

The sky was blushing in shades of orange and pink.

On the veranda, **Anjali and Vihan sat side by side**, their tea cups warm in their hands, the breeze soft, the laughter of family echoing from downstairs.

No words were needed.
Only quiet smiles.
And a shared peace that said — *we've made it through everything.*

But peace doesn't last long in a house full of loving chaos.

Suddenly, someone called out from the courtyard below:

"Anjali Didi… Vihan Bhaiyaaa! Come down — we have a question!"

Then came another playful voice,

"It's YOUR turn now. You both have exactly 5 minutes to answer — do you want to marry each other or not?"

Laughter followed.

Anjali and Vihan looked at each other, startled.

Both smiled nervously.
Both... unsure.

"What if she's not ready?"
"What if he still needs time?"

Their hearts raced, but they didn't speak.

Just then, one of the new damaads, smiling ear to ear, came upstairs with a pen and two pieces of paper.

"Let's settle this like grown-ups," he said with a wink.
"You both write your answer — don't show it. If your words match, we'll consider it fate."

Everyone downstairs clapped and hooted.

Two Notes, One Answer

Vihan held the pen first.

He stared at the blank paper for a few seconds, then wrote slowly:

"I'm ready… if Anjali is."

He folded the note and placed it down.

Anjali, calm on the outside but nervous within, took the pen and quietly wrote:

"I'm ready… if Vihan is."

She looked at him. He looked at her.

They said nothing — because **their silence had always been louder than words.**

The damaad took both notes and read them aloud.

And in that moment — with laughter below, the sunset above, and years of distance now dissolved — **the entire house erupted in cheers.**

The Engagement, The Wait, The Forever

Vihan's parents were called.
The elders from both sides blessed the union.
And in a simple, soulful ceremony — Anjali and Vihan exchanged rings.

No DJ. No grand announcement.

Just a quiet moment, where **two people who had broken and rebuilt themselves** stood side by side… ready.

But they didn't rush into the wedding.

"Let's wait," Anjali said.
"I have my promotion coming. So does he. We need to settle a few things."

The families respected that.

And so, **two years passed** — in calm, in growth, in deepening understanding.

Anjali rose in her role, stronger than ever.

Vihan, now known across departments for his reforms and sincerity, was equally focused.

But through it all — they were together.

Walking. Planning. Living. Loving.

Chapter 26: The Final Chapter — The Wedding of Patience

Two years later, the house once again bloomed with mogra, lights, and shankh sounds.

But this time, the bride was **Anjali**.

Her sisters — now mothers — arrived holding their toddlers, laughing like the girls they once were.

Yatharva, now 4, walked proudly down the aisle in a sherwani, holding the varmala on a silver tray.

He had his father now.

And the house had its eldest damad.

Vihan stood, calm and proud, watching Anjali walk toward him — in a temple-silk saree, no makeup, just that same bindi and watch.

And in his eyes… only one thing lived:

"We made it. Finally. Fully. Forever."

Final Chapter Conclusion: A Dance Before Forever

Just before the **saat phere**, when everything was set — the varmala placed, the mandap glowing in diya light, and the priest preparing for the vows — someone from the crowd shouted:

"Arey shaadi se pehle DJ toh banta hai!"

Laughter exploded.

The cousins clapped, the aunties cheered, and Anjali's sisters ran to her side saying:

"Didi! This is your last night as a bride… come on, one performance is a must!"

Even Anjali blushed.

And then… the courtyard turned into a mini sangeet.

The Family's Final Show of Love

Anjali and her sisters stepped in first.

Wearing their temple-border sarees and jasmine gajras, they danced on a soulful folk song — graceful, rhythmic, full of memories. Each step was a silent story of their journey together.

Then the husbands joined — including Vihan, of course — and did a fun, slightly awkward but adorable group performance choreographed by the sisters earlier.

The surprise?

Anjali's **parents and Tau ji** had been secretly rehearsing a small act for days — planned by the damaads and sisters behind her back.

When they stepped onto the floor to perform a light-hearted family skit mixed with dance — the crowd went *wild* with laughter and love.

Even Anjali got teary-eyed watching them, hand in hand, dancing like they were young again.

The Last Group Photo

After the fun and dance, **the whole family gathered for one big group photo.**

Anjali, Vihan, Yatharva in the center.
The sisters, their husbands, babies, cousins all around.
Parents and elders standing proudly behind.

And just before the photo clicked, **Anjali's father spoke softly but clearly:**

"Finally... the family is complete."

There was a pause. Everyone smiled.

Then he added with a wink:

"Mujhe lagta hai ab Anjali ki maa, main, aur Tau ji teerth yatra nikal jaayein."
(*"I think now Anjali's mother, Tau ji, and I should head for pilgrimage."*)

Laughter erupted again, light-hearted and pure.

Click.

The camera flashed.
The moment froze forever.

www.ingramcontent.com/pod-product-compliance
Lightning Source LLC
Chambersburg PA
CBHW062141160726
48282CB00027B/897
9789334365740